NOT ANOTHER ONE-NIGHT STAND

Not Another Romance Novel

R.L. KENDERSON

Not Another One-Night Stand

Chapter One

PAISLEY

I STARED down at my text and tapped my phone.

"Paisley, what's wrong?" Tessa asked.

Raising my head, I saw six sets of eyes on me. It was another monthly dinner with my friends from high school. We'd all met when we were in choir together and stayed close even though high school was years ago.

I set my phone down. "You know how my landlord is selling the house I rent?"

They nodded their heads. They already knew this from our dinner last month.

"I found another place to live and was ready to sign the papers, but someone beat me to it." I sighed. "Figures."

"Oh, Paise, that sucks," Bree said.

"Yeah. I've actually been thinking that maybe it's time I buy something. I can afford it, and I feel like losing this rental is a sign. Finding a good house to rent can be hard, and I refuse to go back to apartment living." I shuddered.

"So, does this mean it's living with the parents after all?" Pru asked.

I glanced at my phone again and reread the message there. "That's the thing. My sister's brother-in-law is out of the country. He has a house just sitting there, empty. He had a house sitter for a couple months, but that person moved out. Audrey said it would be the perfect place for me to stay while I looked for a house to buy, and I wouldn't have to pay rent."

"What's holding you back?" Elizabeth asked.

My friends knew me so well.

"I've never met the guy. It seems strange to live in someone's house when I don't know him at all."

"Didn't you meet him at your sister's wedding?" Isabelle asked.

I shook my head. "They eloped while they were on vacation."

"Oh, that's right."

Tessa tapped her chin. "I don't think it matters too much if you've never met him. He's family of family. You like your brother-in-law, right?"

"Yes. He's a great guy." My sister got lucky with him.

"And your sister loves you. She's not going to send you to live someplace bad. Plus, the guy is out of the country. You won't have a landlord breathing down your neck. And that's basically what he is if he's not there. A landlord," Tessa pointed out.

I laughed. My current landlord was okay, but he did like to show up, unannounced, sometimes. Or he used to be okay. He'd failed to tell me he was selling the house I'd been living in for years until it was almost too late.

"It feels really weird to know I'd be living with his things. I've never lived in a place furnished by someone else."

Bree waved her hand at my concern. "You can absolutely get used to the furniture. But Tessa's right. You really have nothing to lose. You get to live there for free, you don't have to sign a lease, and it'll give you time and money to look for your own place to buy."

"And if you're still worried, warn your sister that if this guy is a slob or a creep, you are going to move in with her." Pru winked. "That should convince her to tell you the truth."

I laughed. "Good idea. I'm going to call her after dinner and tell her I'm going to do it."

Just saying the words lifted a huge weight off my shoulders.

"Enough about me. What's going on in everyone else's lives?"

Last time the United She-Woman Single Ladies with Our Vibrators So We Never Have Another Bad Date or Experience Romance Again Because Men Suck Club had gotten together, one of us had gotten married and another engaged.

"Isabelle, are you still dating that guy?"

She shrugged. "Yeah, I'm not sure we're going to keep seeing each other though. He's been kind of distant lately."

Alexis squeezed her hand. "I'm sorry."

I was sure that Alexis probably knew exactly how that felt, except it had been with her ex-husband.

Everyone else looked as concerned as I felt, except Elizabeth. Elizabeth almost looked excited. I knew the two were closer to each other than the rest of us, and maybe she thought this guy wasn't good enough for Isabelle.

For my friends, most of them were done with dating—or had been until recently—because they were sick of the men out there. It was the reason we had started the United She-Woman Single Ladies with Our Vibrators So We Never Have Another Bad Date or Experience Romance Again Because Men Suck Club. But with me, I was more of the villain in the relationship than the victim.

I had a history of getting attached to a guy way too fast, which often scared them off. And while our club's unofficial rule was *no dating*, there was nothing about sex, except for when it came to me.

I liked sex a lot, but that also played directly into my problem with falling for someone who didn't want to get serious.

My last failed relationship was someone I'd met on a dating app. He had been up front about being casual, and I'd thought I could handle that. But I started to want more and got clingy. By the end, he'd called me a stalker and kicked me out of his place.

After that, I had started sleeping with a guy friend that I thought would be just my fuck buddy. But I'd developed feelings for him, and he hadn't felt the same.

As you could guess, we were no longer friends. And to make matters worse, he was now engaged, and I was very, very single.

So, yes, I was the one who always seemed to get rejected, but I was also the one who broke the rules and pursued men when they didn't want to be. At least, not by me, and that was why I was more villain than victim. Or maybe I was both, except the person I hurt was myself because the guys who didn't want to get serious with me didn't suffer from broken hearts.

Either way, I really missed sex sometimes, but I supposed it was better than crying into my pillow every night.

———

After hugging all my friends, I left the restaurant and went to my car to call my sister.

"Hello?"

"Hey, it's me," I said.

"I was wondering what happened to you. You never texted me back."

"Yeah, I had to think about it."

"What's to think about? It's a house, it's free, and it's empty."

I chuckled. "Yeah, that's pretty much what my friends said."

"Your friends are right."

"What is Felix's brother like? He's not a weirdo or anything, is he? Because if I find a dead body in the basement, I'm moving in with you."

Audrey laughed. "He's perfectly normal, and I've been to his house a couple of times. I've also been in the basement. It's finished with no dead bodies."

That was a relief.

"Seriously, Paise, I would not offer this to you if I thought it was a bad idea."

"When is Felix's brother supposed to come back? You said he's out of the country for work?"

"Yes. CJ went over there to work on a yearlong project. He has a little less than four months left. That's probably enough time for you to find someplace different, right?"

It would be a tight squeeze to find a house to buy, but it would absolutely give me enough time to find another place to rent.

"I think so."

"Look at your phone," my sister said.

I put her on speaker and pulled up my text messages.

"What are these?" I asked.

"They are pictures of Felix and me when we were hanging out at CJ's. Obviously, we were taking pics of ourselves, but you can see the house in the background."

I flipped through the four she'd sent me. From what I could see, it was a decent house.

"Are there any pictures of CJ?"

"I looked through my phone and didn't find any.

Sorry." She lowered her voice. "But CJ is even hotter than Felix. Don't tell the hubby I said that."

"I won't." I really liked my brother-in-law, and he was good to my sister, but he was not what I would call hot, so the chances of CJ being hot seemed slim to none. But I wasn't going to say that out loud to my sister. "And it doesn't really matter what he looks like as long as he's not a serial killer."

"Hmm...now that you say that, the statistics on the murders of young redheads have dropped since he left the country."

"Ha-ha-ha," I told my sister. "If that were true, you'd be in more trouble than me."

"How so? We're both gingers."

"Proximity. Why would he murder me when he could murder you?"

"Fair point. So, it's a good thing he's obviously not a serial killer."

"Does he have a girlfriend?"

"Uh...I'm trying to follow the path from serial killer to girlfriend."

I laughed. "They're unrelated. I was just thinking, I don't want a jealous girlfriend to think I'm coming after her man."

"Oh, that makes sense. No, he's single. Unless he met someone overseas. But then she'd be far away and she wouldn't even know about you."

"You know just how to make a girl feel comfortable."

"That's what I'm here for. So, should I tell Felix to let his brother know that you'll be staying there?"

I took a deep breath and exhaled. "Yeah, sure. Why the hell not?"

It was just a few months. It wasn't like it was going to change my life or anything.

Chapter Two

COLIN

I EXITED the plane with my carry-on bag. I had packed light, so I wouldn't have to bother checking my luggage because I hated being at the airport any longer than I had to be. Also, when I had first packed for my trip back to the US, I had been eager to go to the home I hadn't seen in eight and a half months.

When I had started my job years ago, I'd loved traveling. It was one of the reasons I'd wanted to work for the company. But after doing it for so long, it was getting old, and this recent assignment was the longest I had ever been on. I'd been in the UK for nearly three-quarters of a year, and I still had over three months to go, which was why I was excited to be back home even if only for a few days.

But that was before my brother called and left me a message that he was letting a family member of his wife's move in. Felix's voice mail had cut in and out, so I'd missed who exactly was living in my house now, but it didn't matter because I didn't want to go home and spend time with a stranger. It would be awkward for both of us. I was only in town for a few days for work before I went back to the UK, and I didn't want to spend that time making small talk with someone I'd just met.

I walked out of the airport just as my Uber pulled up to take me to a hotel. It wasn't my first choice, but at least I would get to be alone, and it was closer to my work. And the next time I came back to the States for good, my house would be all mine again.

―――――

I dropped off my luggage in my hotel room and left to get a drink down at the hotel bar. Minnesota was six hours behind the UK, so it was the middle of the night there, but I had slept on the plane, and I wasn't ready to call it a night yet. I was hoping a little bit of alcohol would help me get some rest.

It was a Saturday night, so the bar was decently full but not too crowded, which I appreciated. I found a seat in the corner of the bar, where there were several empty stools. I was nursing my first drink when I saw her walk in.

She was average height, and the word *pretty* came to mind when describing her. But it was the red hair that really caught my eye. It was almost wild with curls going everywhere. She was dressed up, but she looked more like she was going to work rather than on a date, and she was alone. Her makeup was light, and her black dress had a modest neckline and three-quarter sleeves. The sexiest piece of clothing on her was her red heels.

She looked around, and I realized I might have been wrong. She could be meeting someone there, and maybe she liked to dress more conservatively for dates. Except her eyes scanned over all the people, and she only stopped when they landed on the empty stools next to me.

Her expression brightened, and she came and took the stool two away from mine. She gave me a polite smile, and I nodded in return before the bartender came over and took her drink order.

We both sat there, minding our own business for a good ten minutes before laughter had me looking up again. A group of women who I guessed to be in their mid-fifties walked in. And the redhead next to me stiffened. She slunk off her stool—there was no other way to describe it—and walked around to my side, facing the wall.

"I'm sorry to ask this," she whispered. "But can you move over one seat and let me take this spot? I'm hoping that won't be for long, but I would really appreciate it."

I moved over silently and let her take my old seat.

She sat down with a sigh. "Thank you."

"You're welcome." I tilted my head toward the ladies. "Not your friends, I take it?"

The redhead smiled. "I'm here for an office party. I just wanted to take a break for a little while, have a drink, and get away from everyone."

That explained the clothes and makeup. She actually was dressed for work instead of a night out.

I looked at the group of ladies, who were finding a table that, unfortunately, put the redhead and me in their line of view. I leaned forward, putting my elbows on the bar so that, hopefully, they wouldn't notice she was sitting next to me.

"So, those must be your coworkers?" I asked.

"Yes. The four of them work in the same area as me. They're nice enough, but they're not exactly the people I want to hang out with on a Saturday night." She chuckled. "That probably sounds mean, especially to someone who doesn't know me. I swear, I'm not a monster."

I offered her a reassuring smile. "I think we've all been there." I worked with several people who I wouldn't want to spend my time off with outside of work.

"Thank you. I'm the youngest of all of them by about twenty years. We're not at the same point in our lives, and they've all been working at the company a lot longer than me. Like I said, they're not my first pick of who I'd want to hang out with on a Saturday night." She took a sip of her drink. "Actually, I feel that way about my whole office. I work at a boring insurance company, so tonight's party isn't what I would call fun." She grinned. "Are you judging me yet?"

I laughed. "You don't have to justify anything to me. I'm just a stranger you met at the bar." But I felt like I needed to remedy that. I held out my hand. "I'm Colin, by the way."

―――――

PAISLEY

I smiled and said, "I'm Paisley," as I shook his hand.

Colin had blue eyes and blond hair and was the kind of guy most girls had a crush on in high school, including me. No surprise there. I'd had a crush on tons of guys in high school. I was me after all.

But being around someone so hot was not good for me and my *no men, no sex* rule.

Although...

"So, Colin, what brings you here tonight? Is it something as exciting as the sixtieth anniversary of your company being open?"

He grinned, which only made him more attractive. "I'm here for my job, too, and I actually have to do some work on Monday but nothing as exciting as an anniversary party." He snickered.

"You think you're funny, but if you had to be in that room with everyone from my office, you'd see how much work it actually is. And I'm not even getting paid for it."

He burst out laughing, and I wanted to give myself a pat on the back for making this beautiful man happy, if only for a moment.

He leaned closer to me. "You know, Paisley, I was regretting coming into town for a few days, but you might just change my mind."

"Might?"

He lifted his glass and emptied it. "We'll see how the rest of the night goes," he said, meeting my eyes.

Now that I knew he was only going to be in town for a few days, I had a good feeling on how the night would go.

It was going to end with the both of us naked.

Chapter Three

COLIN

PAISLEY PUSHED me up against the door to my hotel room, pressed her body against mine, and grinned.

"You're a wild one, aren't you?"

She tilted her head. "Why do you say that? My hair?"

She was still smiling at me, but I sensed it wasn't as genuine.

Is this a test? It didn't matter because it wasn't going to change my answer.

"No. It's the glint in your eye. I've never had someone tell me we were going to end the night by getting naked after only a few minutes of conversation."

Chuckling, she said, "To be fair, I thought I was thinking that in my head. I didn't know I had said it out loud."

I cupped her ass as I yanked her closer, so I could rub her cleft over my hardness. "To be fair, it completely turned me on."

After I'd practically been kicked out of my own house, having sex with this woman would go a long way to making me feel better.

"Then, why do we still have our clothes on?"

I set Paisley away from me and stripped off my clothes in ten seconds flat.

Her eyes widened. "Holy shit," she whispered.

I looked down at my body to try to see what she was looking at, but I didn't notice anything.

I ran my hands over my chest and abs, and then I cupped my hard cock to make sure I wasn't missing something.

"Oh my God, stop."

I lifted my head. "What's wrong?"

She waved her hands in front of her face. "I think I might come just from seeing you naked. And watching you touch yourself like that. I can't handle it."

I grinned. That was the opposite of something being wrong.

I stepped forward and pulled her into my arms. "Then, you'd better get naked so that I can catch up to you." I unzipped her dress and stepped back, so I could get a good view.

The material hit the floor, and she stood in front of me in a lacy black bra with matching panties. And red high heels.

"Fuck me. I'm already there."

She licked her bottom lip and threw her arms around my neck. I kissed her as I maneuvered us over to the bed.

Finding the back of her bra, I unclasped it and dragged it off her arms.

We fell onto the bed, and I sucked in one pink nipple between my lips. Her back arched, and she threw a leg around me, so I continued to pay attention to her breasts. I slipped my hand underneath her panties to find her ready, and I groaned. Nothing was better than wet pussy.

I was ready to play, wanting to get her off the first time with my hand, but she suddenly pushed me away.

"Whaaa..." I started but cut myself off when I saw what Paisley was doing.

She kicked off her heels and drew her panties down her legs. There was something so sensual about watching a woman take off her underwear.

Now that we were both naked, it occurred to me that we might need a condom—and soon. Thankfully, my bag was on the other side of the mattress.

I scooted up, unzipped my side pocket, and reached inside. Just as my hand found my prize, I looked up to see Paisley kneeling over me on the bed. I liked a woman whose ideas followed mine in the bedroom.

But she wasn't thinking sex. At least, not *penis in vagina* sex.

She was thinking oral sex based on where she was sitting.

And I wasn't going to complain one bit.

She grabbed on to my cock and stroked me a few times. I was already so horny that I could feel pre-cum escape out of my dick. I waited for Paisley to do what most women did. Wipe it off or change their mind. But she squeezed my head until more leaked forth and licked it off.

"Fuck."

Paisley kissed the tip and sucked my length into her mouth and down her throat like a pro. I was the one who practically choked...on my own tongue.

I tried to lie back and let her do her thing, but her mouth felt incredible, and soon, I was thrusting my hips. Trying to stop myself from what came naturally was an exercise in self-control.

Paisley slid off my lap and onto the floor. I was still hard, and my balls were ready to explode, so I almost didn't hear what she said.

"Fuck my mouth."

I blinked. "What?"

"Fuck my mouth." She smirked at me. "I know you want to."

"Hell yeah, I want to. It's just..."

"You won't hurt me. I like it."

I could either be a gentleman and tell her *no, thank you* even though I wanted to really bad or I could say screw it and make this the best one-nighter I'd had in a long time.

"Are you sure?" I couldn't help asking.

She leaned forward, and as she pulled me back into her mouth, she nudged my hips toward her. That was all the coaxing I needed. I moved to the end of the bed and cupped her head. She opened her mouth, and I slid my cock inside. I started slow and didn't thrust too hard, but I noticed the more I let go, the louder Paisley's moans got.

Fuck me. She was into it as much as I was.

After that, I didn't hold back, and I fucked her mouth just like she wanted.

And when my nuts tightened, I told her, "I'm going to come now," shortly before I yanked her close and came down her throat.

I had to give myself a few seconds before I could see or think again; the post-orgasmic haze was so strong.

I released Paisley from my grip and hauled her up into my arms.

I gently pushed her back onto the bed and spread her legs wide. After she'd given me the best blow job I'd had in years, I wanted to return the favor. I also wanted to see how she tasted, and if I was being fully honest, I needed the extra recovery time.

But before I could get down on my knees, she arched up enough to grab me around the neck and pull me closer to her. "I need it. Please. I need it. It's been so long."

"Need what, baby?"

"Your cock."

Now, I knew she wasn't talking about *my* dick specifically because we had just met. But it still got me harder than stone. My recovery time went way down when a sexy woman talked dirty to me.

I picked up the condom I had thrown on the bed and hastily put it on before lining myself up at her entrance. I looked up to her eyes as she licked her lips.

"Please go slow," she said as her breathing quickened.

I wasn't the biggest guy in the world, but I wasn't the

smallest either, and since she had hinted at the fact that it had been a while, I didn't want to hurt her, so I did as the lady had requested.

Ever so slowly, I guided my cock inside her as I ran my hands up her sides and cupped her breasts. I flicked her nipples as I reached the hilt. I was taken completely by surprise when I felt her pussy tighten around me, and an extended sigh escaped past her lips while her eyes rolled back in her head as they closed.

"Holy shit. Did you just come?"

Paisley chuckled. It was the kind of laugh one did when they almost couldn't believe something had just happened. "Oh, yeah. It's why I wanted you to take your time."

Even though the woman was tight, it hadn't been about my size, but about the experience, which was somehow sexier.

"Amazing," I whispered.

I gradually pulled out and pushed back in to see if I could get the same response out of her.

Remarkably, it happened again. As I drove forward, she squeezed my dick, and instead of a sigh this time, a small mewing sound came from the back of her throat.

Chapter Four

PAISLEY

I WOKE WITH A START, knowing right away that I had fallen asleep in Colin's hotel room.

Shit.

When I'd granted myself permission to get my freak on, I'd told myself that I was not allowed to fall back into my old habits, which included falling asleep in the guy's bed.

Falling asleep led to cuddling, and cuddling led to feelings. At least, it did for me.

I gently slid out from underneath Colin's arm so as not to wake him and pushed myself off the bed. I turned around and let myself look at him. He had moved to his back after I left, and the sheet was hanging off his hips.

Not only was he good in bed, but he was gorgeous too. Muscular but not too much, and his dick was perfect. It didn't hurt that he'd tasted amazing.

Clenching my jaw, I forced myself to look away. If I kept staring at Colin, I was going to do something stupid, like wake him up and ask for his last name or phone number or leave mine for him to find after he woke up.

I needed to focus.

The clock on the nightstand said it was after one a.m. That was good. I hadn't been there all night. That bit of news helped me stick to my plan.

I tiptoed to the bathroom to use the facilities and to check myself in the mirror before I might run into other people. I cringed at what I saw there.

My hair was a curly mess, and my makeup was smudged. My eyes were black underneath from when they'd watered as I gave Colin a blow job. As good as it had been, I maybe should have held off from doing things that would make me look like a racoon when I knew I was going to have to go home eventually.

I shrugged. *It was worth it.*

But since there was no way I could fix my makeup, I used some of the free hotel soap and washed the evidence of great sex from my face.

When I opened the door, I was surprised to find Colin standing there, leaning against the doorframe.

He smiled and pulled me into his arms. "Everything okay?"

Well, I had planned to leave without saying good-bye, but feeling his naked body pressed up to mine had me changing my mind. He had sought me out, so it didn't count if I returned to his bed, right?

I slid my arms up and around his neck. "I'm better now that you're awake."

His penis thickened against my stomach. "Good. Because I'm not done with you yet."

———

Colin's breathing evened out, and I willed myself to stay awake. It was hard when I was in a warm bed, next to a warm body, and there was the promise of more great sex awaiting me if I stayed.

But I was determined to not fail the assignment I'd given myself.

I managed to use the bathroom, get dressed, and get out of the hotel room without a peep from Colin.

The hotel was quiet with only one person behind the desk as I left. When I got to my car, I finally noticed the time and saw that it was almost four in the morning. I had stayed longer than I'd planned, but at least the sun wasn't up.

When I got home a half hour later, I showered all traces of sex off my body and crawled into bed.

But before I let myself fall asleep, I found my message thread with Bree, Tessa, Isabelle, Alexis, Pru, and Elizabeth and sent them a text.

Me: I met a guy in the hotel bar tonight and had sex with him. I'm home now. I left before he woke up, and I didn't ask for his phone number or even his last name. I think I deserve a pat on the back.

I went to set my phone down, figuring all my friends were sleeping, but it vibrated in my hand.

Tessa: I'm proud of you, but what if you get pregnant or a disease? Shouldn't you be able to track him down?

Bree: Don't be a mood killer, Tessa. She knows what hotel he's staying at and what room. If she needs to find him, she can track him down. I had plenty of one-nighters where I never exchanged phone numbers or last names. She'll be fine.

Bree: Way to go, Paisley. You got some, and you didn't fall for the guy.

Tessa: I was worried, so sue me.

Bree: I know. Love you!

Me: Thank you both. Thanks, Tessa, for worrying about me, but I'm fine. And thanks, Bree. I am kind of proud of myself.

Bree: You should be. Now, if you can, promise to not go back there and track him down tomorrow.

Me: I'm not going to do that.

Tessa: If you need me to babysit you, I can do that. ;-)

Me: I thought you were against the one-night stand?

Tessa: No. Just didn't want you to not be able to find him if you needed to.

Me: We used condoms. I might fall for men, but I always practice safe sex.

Bree: At least one of us does.

I laughed out loud. I knew that Bree was teasing Tessa for getting pregnant.

Tessa: You're so funny, Bree. But I'm now happily married, so I can't complain.

Bree: Very true.

Me: What are the two of you doing up at this time?

Tessa: I was hungry. This baby keeps me eating 24/7.

Bree: Sex. No one told me that getting engaged to a manwhore who'd changed his ways meant that I'd have to keep up with his insatiable sex drive. Don't tell Zack, but sometimes, my pussy is sore after doing it all weekend. I actually don't mind going to work because I get a break.

Tessa: I don't want to think about my brother like that.

Me: Why don't you tell him?

Bree: Sorry, Tessa. I don't say anything because not only do I not want to hurt his feelings, but he also gives me the best orgasms. Plus, I'm not usually sore until Monday morning. To be fair, I don't know when to stop any more than he does.

I understood the *best orgasms* part. I would totally go to work sore on Monday morning if I got to have more sex with Colin.

Nope. Paisley, don't think about him too much.

I might need to take Tessa up on her offer to babysit me tomorrow.

Tessa: Now that I know too much about my brother's sex life, I think it's time for me to go back to bed.

I yawned.

It was probably time for me to go to sleep too. The rest of our friends were going to have a lot of messages to read in the morning as it was.

Me: Yeah, me too.

Bree: Night, ladies.

Tessa: Night.

Me: Night.

Chapter Five

COLIN

SIX WEEKS LATER

I WAS HAVING déjà vu as I got off the plane, except this time, I was back for good. And I didn't have to go to a hotel. I was going home. I still wasn't excited about having someone live with me, but I was the one who'd finished my project early, and my brother had promised me that my roommate would not be living there forever.

Felix was waiting for me down at baggage claim and grinned when he saw me.

"Hey," he yelled and held out his arms.

I grabbed my brother in a bear hug and yanked him to my chest. Despite him telling a stranger that they could live in my house, I'd really missed the guy.

We pounded each other's backs and separated.

"Where's Audrey?" I asked. "I thought you said both of you were going to come."

"I dropped her off at your house. Since we're going to introduce you to your houseguest anyway, she decided to skip the airport."

I didn't blame her. I was getting sick of airports myself.

"Who did you say moved in again?"

Felix's eyes widened.

"Your voice mail didn't come through very clear."

"So, you've been letting someone you don't know live at your house?"

"No. *You've* been letting someone I don't know live at my house."

Felix chuckled. "True."

"And I know it's a relative of Audrey's. I just didn't catch who it was."

"I guess I won't judge you as much for not knowing. It's her sister. Her landlord kicked her out kind of last minute, so she needed a place to stay." He leaned in close and lowered his voice. "And do not tell Audrey this, but I wasn't going to let her sister stay with us."

I raised my eyebrows. "If my place is trashed, you're paying for it."

"No, man, she's not irresponsible. She's just...kind of annoying sometimes. She doesn't have a filter on her."

This was good news and bad news. I didn't have to worry about my furniture being ruined, but I would have to live with someone who was irritating.

"Great," I said sarcastically.

"You'll be fine. You're not much different." Felix pointed as he looked over my shoulder. "Luggage is here."

"What do you mean, I'm not much different?" I asked, but my brother was already five steps ahead of me, and with the people and the carousel moving, he didn't hear a word I'd said.

By the time we got my two large suitcases and got to Felix's car, we had moved on to a new subject, and I forgot about my new, possibly annoying houseguest.

When we got to my place, Felix parked in the driveway, next to Audrey's car, and I didn't see another around, which meant that either the sister wasn't there or she was parked in my garage.

"I forgot to tell you that Audrey picked up your favorite."

I perked up. "Broder's?"

"You know it."

My mouth was already watering. Broder's Pasta Bar had the best Italian food. I had planned to go and eat there when I was in town six weeks ago, but I'd run out of time. It had been over a year, and now, my mind was solely on food.

Felix helped me bring in my stuff, and I couldn't help but grin when I walked in the door. There was nothing like being home.

Audrey was setting the table in the kitchen and smiled when she saw me. "Hey, stranger." She came over and hugged me.

"Hey yourself. It smells great in here."

"I would like to say it's all me, but all I did was drive to the restaurant and back."

"I heard you got my favorite," I said with an expectant smile.

Audrey laughed at me. "I did."

"I can't wait." I looked around. "I suppose we have to wait for my new houseguest before we eat?"

"Yes."

"I guess it is the polite thing to do," I said with a smile even though I wasn't very excited about living with anyone. I liked walking around naked and doing anything else I wanted without someone watching.

"Especially since you were the one who cut your trip short."

I held up my hands. "First of all, it wasn't a trip. It was an assignment. And we finished early. It can't be helped."

And even though I did have to share my place with someone, I was glad to be home.

"Well, I'm happy to have you back," Felix said.

"Thanks, bro. I'm going to check out this food while I wait though."

As I headed into the kitchen, my sister-in-law said something that had me stopping in my tracks. "As soon as Paisley comes out of her bedroom, we can eat."

I spun around on my heel and cleared my throat. "Did you say Paisley?"

There was no way it could be my Paisley. It wasn't a very common name, but it wasn't completely unique either.

Audrey blinked. "Yes. Paisley. My sister." Her brow furrowed. "Have you two already met?"

"I don't think—"

"Audrey, did you call for me?" a voice said from the other side of the wall as I strained to see if it sounded familiar.

My sister-in-law, who was standing in a place to see both sides, turned her head toward the speaker. "Yeah, I was just telling CJ that we had to wait for you before we could eat."

"He's here?"

Audrey nodded and pointed toward me. "He's in the kitchen."

"Hey, CJ. It's—" Paisley froze as soon as she came around the corner and saw me standing there.

My brother, who had been off to the side, watching the whole time, stepped forward and eyed us both. "Do you two know each other?"

Paisley crossed her arms across her chest. "No," she said, her eyes full of anger.

"Paisley, this is CJ Black. CJ, this is my sister, Paisley Davis," Audrey said, clearly not reading the room.

Frowning, I ignored my sister-in-law and homed in on Paisley's response. *No?* The hell we didn't know each other. I knew her well enough to know what her pussy felt like, wrapped around my cock, while I made her come.

And why the hell was she mad at me? She was the one who had snuck out of my room while I was sleeping, never to be heard from again. She wasn't the one left behind, wanting more.

For a month and a half, I'd been thinking about this

woman and how I wanted her in my bed again because one night hadn't been enough, and now, she was pretending like she didn't know me.

If we were alone, I would yank her into my arms and kiss her to remind her how good we were together.

Just like that, having a roommate didn't seem so bad.

"He does look like a guy I met a while back. His name was Colin though," Paisley said, and suddenly, it clicked.

I started laughing, confusing Felix and Audrey, while Paisley shot daggers at me. It took me a few seconds to compose myself, but when I did, I held out my hand. "Hi, Paisley. It's nice to meet you again. I'm Colin, but my family, including my sister-in-law, calls me CJ. It stands for Colin Jasper."

Paisley's arms fell to her sides, and her face turned red. Her eyes were big, and she looked away.

I reached forward and picked up her hand that was dangling at her side and lowered my voice. "I didn't mean to embarrass you. The name thing can be confusing."

She looked up, a shameful expression all over her face. "I'm sorry."

"No sorry needed. Not for the name thing anyway." I leaned closer and whispered, "But you still owe me an apology for leaving me to wake up all alone in my room before I got to fuck you again."

Chapter Six

PAISLEY

I GASPED and quickly pulled my hand from Colin's handshake before he felt the sweat on my palm.

I had been nervous about meeting my new roommate and the man whose house I was living in, yet I *never* expected it to be the guy I'd had a one-night stand with a month and a half ago.

Shocked didn't even begin to explain how I felt.

I had been so proud of myself for not getting his phone number and not tracking him down later. And here I was, living in his house.

Fate was a cruel bitch.

Watching Colin, or CJ, or whatever his name was as he dished up his food and sat down at the table had me really reflecting on my life decisions.

He seemed unfazed by the two of us meeting up again in this crazy situation. Meanwhile, hiding in my room sounded like a better idea than sitting here and pretending like everything was normal. But if I didn't eat, my sister and brother-in-law were going to wonder what was wrong with me.

"Why don't you go next, Paisley?" Audrey offered.

I smiled politely and dished up as little food as possible without someone questioning my eating habits. But then came the hard part. Should I sit across from him, which was the farthest I could sit, and force myself to look at him face-to-face? Or should I sit next to him, so I wouldn't have to look at him?

Damn round table. I needed a huge dining room, so I could sit far, far away.

After everyone was seated, Felix asked, "So, how did you two meet?"

My eyes darted to Colin, but he was looking at his brother. "We met at a hotel bar."

Audrey was sitting across from me, and she frowned at me. "What were you doing at a hotel bar?"

"I was there for my work party."

"Oh, that's right." She looked at Colin. "What were you doing there?"

"Yeah, why weren't you in England?" Felix asked.

Colin glanced my way for a second, a guilty look in his eyes. "I had to come back for a few days for work, and..." He cleared his throat. "And since you had offered to let Paisley move in, I thought it would be easier to stay at a hotel."

What little appetite I had left vanished.

I was the reason he hadn't come home. I felt awful.

But apparently, I was the only one who felt guilty.

Felix shrugged. "Sorry, dude. I didn't know, or I would have told Paisley to wait to move in."

Colin shrugged too. It must have been a family trait. "No biggie." He looked my way again, but this time, he smiled, heat in his eyes. "It was worth it."

Immediately, my face warmed. I picked up the glass of water sitting in front of me and downed half of it.

"So, you two didn't figure out who you were to each other?" Audrey asked.

Colin smirked. "It didn't come up."

Oh God.

"You told me his name was CJ. He told me his name was Colin," I explained in my defense. "How was I to know they were the same person?"

Audrey waited a beat. "Okay, I'll give you that." She turned to Colin. "But how did you not put Paisley together?"

"Because your darling husband called me when he had bad reception, and all I got out of the voice mail he'd left me was that it was a member of your family."

My sister's mouth dropped open as she swung to face Felix. "You left him a voice mail? Didn't you think it was important to actually talk to your brother and see if it was okay that Paisley lived here?"

Felix had just shoved a bite of food into his mouth, so we all waited for him to chew and swallow before speaking. "I didn't think it was that big of a deal. They're both family." He looked at his brother. "Sorry."

"It's fine." Colin looked at me. "Everything is working out the way it's supposed to, I think."

I had no idea what he meant by that, but I was ready to be done with this weird family dinner we had going on.

I finished my pasta and stood.

"What are you doing?" Audrey asked.

"I'm tired, and I have to work tomorrow. I think I'm going to go to bed."

"But you hardly ate anything. And what about dessert? I got cake."

Damn her. She knew I loved cake.

I could always sneak a piece later.

"That sounds great, but I'm really full. I had a big lunch. Save me some, okay?"

I didn't wait for a response. I just carried my dishes to the sink, cleaned them off, and stuck them in the dishwasher.

"Good night, Audrey. Good night, Felix." I forced myself to make eye contact with Colin. "Welcome home."

"Thanks."

And with that, I spun on my heel and headed to my room. When I had moved in, I had been thankful that the spare room was empty, and I could move in my own bed and some of my other things, allowing me to rent a smaller storage space. Now, I wished I had only brought my clothes.

As soon as I shut the door, I pulled out my laptop and began looking for places to live.

———

Several hours later, I was lying awake and couldn't go to sleep. Every time I closed my eyes, I pictured Colin's face as he'd stood over me in the hotel room. The moment before he pushed inside me and made me come.

I threw a mini tantrum on my bed and sat up.

I had barely thought about this man since I'd last seen him, and now, I couldn't stop thinking about him.

There had to be something I could do to get Colin and sex off the brain. Or at least, sex *with* Colin out of my mind.

Finding my laptop where I had left it on my bed, I turned it on again and went to my preferred porn site. I found a video with my favorite actor, turned the volume down low, and hit play.

After several minutes, I reached into my bedside drawer and grabbed my quietest vibrator. I turned it on and pictured the porn star on my computer screen. Since I had already been in the mood, it didn't take me long to finish, and when I did, I felt better. Especially since I hadn't thought of my new roommate once.

Hopefully, this time, when I closed my eyes, I would be able to sleep.

Chapter Seven

PAISLEY

I TAPPED the side of my coffee cup, willing the coffeemaker to brew faster.

I had slept good for about two hours last night and tossed and turned for the rest. It was only four thirty in the morning, but I had given up on getting more sleep before I had to leave for work.

And if I was going to be awake, I was going to have coffee and cake.

The breakfast of champions for me.

When the coffee was finally done, I carried it and my cake to the living room. I clicked on the television, so I could find some guilty-pleasure TV, rounding out my morning with the perfect threesome.

After finishing my cake and coffee, I lay down and was starting to doze off when I heard footsteps coming down the hall.

I was just sitting up when Colin walked into the room,

wearing only a pair of gray sweatpants. I remembered he had a nice body, but I didn't recall it being that nice. He was gorgeous.

"Oh, hey," he said when he saw me. "I didn't know you were up."

He looked me up and down, and I was quickly reminded that I was wearing baggy pajamas, no makeup, and I hadn't touched my hair after getting out of bed. I was sure I looked nothing like the woman he had taken upstairs to his hotel room.

"I hope I didn't wake you."

"Nah. I'm all over the place with my sleep cycle, thanks to the plane ride and coming from a completely different time zone."

"There's coffee in the kitchen if you want some," I offered.

"Thanks."

As soon as he was out of view, I relaxed. I hoped he would get a cup and go back to his room. I had stayed in my room all night. It was his turn to hide.

But rather than going back down the hall, when Colin came back, he sat down on the couch with me.

"Are you watching *Charmed*?"

"Yes, the original. You know *Charmed*?"

"Yeah."

"Do you watch it?" I knew there were men who watched *Charmed*, but I had never met one.

"Not really. I'm more of a *Supernatural* fan myself."

I pursed my lips. *Figures. Supernatural* was acceptable because the main characters were men and not women.

"But maybe we'll have to watch it together now that we're roomies." Colin turned his attention toward the TV. "We could start with this episode."

One did not start *Charmed* in the middle of season four. And while I appreciated his interest, we had bigger things to discuss than television shows.

I cleared my throat and stiffened my spine. "Speaking of being roomies, I'll get out of here as soon as I can find a place to live. Audrey originally told me I had about four months before you came back, and I didn't know you were moving home until a couple of days ago." I remembered what he had said last night about going to the hotel the night we met instead of coming home. "I'm sure the last thing you want is someone taking up your space."

"What?" He turned and looked at me. "You don't have to move out."

I laughed. "You're not serious, right?"

His brow furrowed. "I am. And I'm not sure why that's funny."

"Colin, we slept together, *and* your brother is married to my sister. If you looked up *awkward* in the dictionary, our situation would be in it."

He took a sip of his coffee and paused. "I have a question for you."

"Okay."

"Do you have a place to live?"

"I mean, no, but—"

"No *buts*. It's either yes or no."

"Okay. No then."

"And what were you planning to do about your living situation before I came back early?"

"I rented before, but I was thinking of buying. I have some money saved up, and I was considering getting a house that needed some work."

I had found it the day before my sister gave me the news about Colin. I had planned to ask around to see how long it would take to fix up and if I could live in it while the work was being completed, but that was before Colin had come home. I definitely didn't have time to buy a fixer-upper now. Unfortunately, my search last night hadn't given me many options either.

"Did you have a house in mind?"

"Kind of. I've only seen it online, so who knows? But it doesn't matter now."

"Why not?"

Is he purposely being this obtuse?

"Because I can't stay here that long." I thought the answer was obvious.

"And why not? I'm not kicking you out."

I was getting frustrated and losing patience. "Colin, you've seen me naked, you've been inside me, and we're not dating. Like I said, it's awkward. You can't possibly want me around."

A grin split over his face, and he laughed. "I see what Felix meant now."

"About what?"

"He said you don't have a filter on you."

My mouth dropped open. "What the hell?"

"Don't let it bug you. I think it's cute."

I crossed my arms across my chest. "That doesn't make me feel better."

He pushed my knee with his foot. "Don't let what my brother said bother you. I'm sure you have things about him you don't love."

Colin did have a point, but I was still mad. And I had to wonder if my sister felt the same way.

"Don't overthink it," Colin said, interrupting my thoughts.

"Easy for you to say. He didn't say it about you."

"I think your living situation is more important than what my pain-in-the-ass brother said."

"I suppose you're right."

"Good, because I have a proposal for you."

"What's that?"

"How about you go and check out that house you like? If it calls to you and you really want it, I'll help you fix it up, and in the meantime, you can stay here as long as you need to."

This seemed too good to be true.

I picked up my dirty dishes and stood. "Why would you offer something like this?" I asked, making sure he heard the speculation in my voice.

"Several reasons."

"And they are?"

"One, you're family of family, and it's the nice thing

to do."

That was a good reason.

"That's one. You said *several*."

"I'm the one who came back to the States early, and I feel bad. I don't want you to feel rushed."

That was considerate of him.

"Okay, that's two." Two was a couple of reasons, not several.

He chuckled to himself and looked away. When he turned back to me, he said, "I don't think I should tell you the third reason."

I scoffed. It couldn't be that bad.

"I can handle it," I assured him.

He shrugged. "Okay. Don't say I didn't warn you." He set down his coffee cup and leaned forward. "It's pretty simple. I want to fuck you again. A lot. And you living here makes that a whole lot more likely to happen."

My eyes widened, and I almost dropped the stuff I was holding. Don't get me wrong. I had been thinking about sex with him again too. I just hadn't expected him to want me back.

He was so sexy, and I couldn't imagine he had any trouble finding women who were interested in him, so I was surprised he would want me again.

His eyes traveled down my body until he stopped at my middle. "I've been thinking about you since we had sex, and one night wasn't nearly enough." He looked back up at me. "So, I'd like a repeat—or several—as long as that works for you."

Chapter Eight

COLIN

PAISLEY'S EYES were huge as she stared at me. She shook her head and said something like, "And Felix thinks I don't have a filter?"

"What?"

"Never mind. I was thinking out loud."

I smiled. She had done that the night we met, and it was one of the things I liked about her. I liked a lot of things about her.

It wasn't like I didn't realize that I barely knew the woman, but my pull to her was more important. I wasn't what I would call a player. I dated women and didn't avoid commitment. But I'd also had several one-night stands. And no one had stuck around in my mind like Paisley had.

And if my mind and body were screaming at me to keep her around, I was going to do my best to try. I couldn't just say good-bye when she might be the future mother of my children. I wanted to get to know her better, and, yes, of course, I wanted to have sex with her again. I was a healthy man after all. But it wasn't just about getting naked.

"Did I scare you?" I asked when she didn't say anything else.

"No," she said slowly as she stared off into space. "I don't really know what I'm thinking, but I know I'm not scared. Confused maybe." She shook her head, as if to clear it. "I can't with this right now," she said and headed to the kitchen.

I jumped off the couch and followed her. "I didn't mean to stress you out."

She laughed as she set her plate in the sink and filled up her cup with more coffee. "You didn't stress me out. I just don't get it."

I leaned against the counter on the opposite side of her to give her space. "What don't you get?"

"I don't know. You. This situation. It's all surreal."

"I suppose it is surreal, but that doesn't make it any less real."

She lifted her mug and took a sip.

"What are you thinking?" *Where's the woman with no filter?* "Are you not interested in me like that?"

Her eyebrow flew up, and I chuckled.

"It's okay if you're not. I understand I'm not everyone's cup of tea. I'm not going to force you to sleep with me or anything."

"No, it's not that."

"Then, what is it?"

Paisley bit her lip and looked away, as if she was trying to collect her thoughts.

I didn't want to pressure her, so I let her take her time and didn't say anything.

When she finally turned back to me, she said, "I need to get ready for work."

Disappointed, I nodded and looked at the clock on the microwave. "I suppose it's about that time, huh?"

She blinked at me. "Yes...it is." She picked up her plate she'd put in the sink and put it in the dishwasher. "Do you have to go to work?"

"I don't have to go in today, but I might swing by to check on things."

She gave me a horrified look. "So, you don't have to go in, but you're going to anyway?"

I laughed. "I like my job. And I have a new project coming up. I'd rather get ahead of any problems."

"I guess I can understand that. What do you do?"

"I'm an architect."

"That's way more exciting than insurance under-writing."

"Hey, we all have jobs that are needed."

She rolled her eyes and picked up her coffee cup. "Thanks for trying to make me feel better," she said as she walked out of the kitchen.

I watched her go and wondered how long she was going to stick around before she moved out.

———

PAISLEY

"Paisley. Paisley."

I heard my name and turned to see who was speaking to me. "I'm sorry. What did you say?"

"I'm going to head to lunch. And you should too. It's almost one."

"*Oh.*" I looked around our area and saw that everyone else was gone. I hadn't even noticed they'd left. A growl erupted from my abdomen. Apparently, my stomach knew it was lunchtime. "Thanks."

"You're welcome."

Janice got up from her cubicle and went toward the break room just as Wendy and Kathleen were coming back.

I locked my computer and stood.

"Are you just going to lunch?" Kathleen asked.

"Yep." I pulled my purse from my desk drawer. "See you in half an hour."

I didn't feel like going to the break room and eating the frozen dinner I had brought for lunch. There were several fast-food restaurants near my work, so I picked one of them to dine from today.

I hadn't told any of my friends yet that my one-night stand was now my roommate, and I'd been debating on if I should tell them at all.

It wasn't that my friends wouldn't be understanding,

and I was sure they'd have plenty of sympathy for me. That wasn't why I wasn't telling them.

It was because I really wanted to take Colin up on his offer.

I didn't want to move out right away to some temporary place, only to move again when I found something I liked. That would be three moves in a matter of months. If I could find my permanent home and move only once more for the next twenty years, I would be very happy.

But the thing was, I also really wanted to sleep with Colin again.

When he'd told me he wanted to fuck me again and that one night wasn't enough, his words had gone straight to my pussy. I almost lay down and let him take me right there on the couch. Thankfully, I had known I had to get ready for work, so he hadn't found out how easy I was. Although since we had already slept together on the night we met, he probably knew I was easy.

But that was the least of my worries. My biggest concern was that I could fall in love with him. And what if we started working on my new house and I couldn't move out? I lived with Colin, and he wouldn't be able to get away from me. I had been called a stalker when all I did was text a guy and stop by his house. I couldn't imagine how Colin would feel if he wanted to avoid me and we lived together.

And the worst of it was that Colin knew my family. When my ex had called me a stalker, I hadn't told anyone. I was so embarrassed, and I feared that my friends would secretly agree with him. But Colin knew my sister and brother-in-law. And my sister would probably tell my parents. I would be horrified if my family thought I was unstable.

As I waited in the drive-through lane for my food, I came to the conclusion that I needed to be up front with him and turn him down. I could just tell him it was one of those *it's me, not you* situations. I was going to be honest about my habit of falling fast and hard for men.

It was a sure way to scare a single guy like him away, and then there would hopefully be no hard feelings between us.

I just hoped he didn't kick me out right away.

Panicking for a moment, I then remembered I had plenty of friends I could crash with and a sister. I didn't really want to live with Audrey and Felix, but maybe Felix would offer to help me with a house.

After eating my lunch in my car, I went back into work.

It crossed my mind that I should text Colin to let him know I wanted to talk, but I remembered I didn't have his phone number. And before I asked my sister, I took a moment to pause and consider what I was about to do.

Texting Colin to tell him I wanted to talk already would make it sound like we were in a relationship, so maybe it was for the best I didn't have his phone number. But if I was going to scare him away, it might be smart to shoot a message over to him.

It was a good thing I was in a *no men* club. I couldn't even decide if I should text my male *roommate*.

As I signed back into my computer, I thought how much easier my life would be if Colin wasn't my sister's brother-in-law or the guy I'd slept with or if he hadn't come back home early.

I thought the universe had it out for me.

Chapter Nine

COLIN

"YOU NEED TO HAVE A PARTY." Mateo clapped his hands so loud that I could hear it through the phone. "Yep, that's it."

"I don't know about that. Aren't we too old to still be having parties?"

My friend scoffed. "We're in our early thirties, not our eighties. We are not too old to have parties. Besides, we're going to keep it small and classy."

I snorted.

"Laugh it up, but I'm not twenty-one, throwing a kegger anymore. I missed you. All our other friends missed you. And we want to have a *welcome home*...get-together."

"Can I think about it?" I asked.

"Sure."

"If I let you do this, where are we having this get-together?"

Mateo lived in a little apartment, so I doubted we would be going to his place.

"I figured we'd have it at your house."

"I should have known."

Mateo laughed.

"Now, I really need to think about it because I'm not alone, and I need to check with my roommate."

As soon as the last word left my mouth, said roommate came through the garage door. I smiled at her from my spot on the couch.

"Roommate?" he asked.

"I told you about that whole thing."

Mateo paused for a few seconds, no doubt searching his memory.

"Oh, that's right."

"Yeah, so it's not only up to me."

"Is she hot?"

"Dude."

"I'm just asking. You know she can come if she wants to."

"I would hope so. She lives here."

Paisley heard this and turned around, a frown on her face.

I pulled the receiver away. "My friend wants to throw a *welcome home* party for me here, but I told him I had to ask you," I explained to her.

She shrugged and opened her mouth.

I slashed my hand in front of my throat several times, but she didn't notice.

"I don't mind. Besides, it's your house," she said loudly.

"*Woohoo*. I heard that. The party is on."

I closed my eyes in defeat.

When I opened them, Paisley mouthed, *I'm sorry.*

It's fine, I mouthed back.

"I'll let you know when it works for me," I told Mateo.

Who didn't respond.

"Mateo."

"What?"

"I *said*, I will let you know when it works for me."

He huffed. "Fine."

"Look, I have to go. We'll talk more about this later."

"Later, dude."

I hit End on my phone and set it on the coffee table.

"I take it, you don't want to have this party?"

I sat up. "I don't know. It would be nice to see every-one, but I'd rather have it somewhere else so that I could leave when I wanted to."

She laughed. "Good plan."

"I try."

Paisley was still standing there, repeatedly shifting from one foot to the other.

"Something on your mind?" I asked.

"I wanted to talk to you about our conversation this morning."

This caught me by surprise. Last night, I had figured her changing the subject was her answer to sleeping with me again.

I patted the cushion seat next to me. "I'm all ears." Or

more accurately, I was all hard-on because as soon as my brain thought I had a chance at having sex with Paisley again, my dick was ready to play.

As she sat, I shifted into a position that covered my crotch and prayed she wouldn't notice.

Paisley faced me and took a deep breath. "First, I want you to know that your offer is very tempting."

"My offer?"

"Yeah. To help me remodel a house."

"Right." I had thought she meant sex.

"And you being an architect, I'm sure you know what you're doing, so it's very enticing."

I kind of knew what I was doing, but I was an architect, not a builder. However, it seemed she was getting ready to tell me no, so it didn't matter.

"But I'm going to have to say no."

And there it was. My rejection.

"Because I want to have sex with you again too."

I perked up. This seemed like the opposite of rejection.

"And even though the offer to help with a house and sleeping with you aren't a package deal..."

It took me a second to realize she was waiting for me to agree.

I cleared my throat. "No, of course not. I would help you with the house even if we weren't sleeping together."

She smiled, and I realized I had been so caught up in my head that I almost blew it with her.

"So, even though they're not a package deal, I know it

would only be so long before I wouldn't be able to resist you."

That made two of us.

I held up a finger to get her to stop for a moment. "I'm sorry, but I don't understand. You want to have sex with me, and I want to have sex with you. Am I missing something?"

"I can't promise I won't fall in love with you," she blurted out.

I laughed until I realized I was the only one. Her face was dead serious.

"The thing is, Colin, I have a big heart, and I fall in love with pretty much every guy I date and sleep with."

"You didn't fall in love with me the night we met."

She chuckled. "That's a rarity, and because of that, I'll probably fall that much faster. And then you'll get annoyed with me."

I was starting to understand that she thought she was going to scare me away with this *falling in love* talk. But I wasn't scared. I was thirty-three. I was ready to meet someone and settle down.

"Why would I get annoyed with you?" I asked.

"Because everyone does." She tried to smile, but I could see that it hurt her.

"I'm sorry that's happened to you."

"You're not supposed to be nice."

I looked around, as if there were someone else in the room to tell me what I was supposed to be. "Uh...I'm not following."

"You're supposed to agree and tell me you want to stay far away from me."

I laughed. "I can't do that."

She turned to face the TV. "This is not going as I planned."

"I'm sorry?"

Her head whipped toward me. "Okay, look. I'm not lying about falling in love with men, but the thing is, I'm trying to stop."

"You're trying not to fall in love? That sounds lonely."

"I don't mean with anybody ever, just not with everybody. I'm trying to be strong and rely on myself a little bit more."

I nodded. I totally understood where she was coming from. I'd had a few friends throughout my life, women and men, who were like this, and I had seen many, many relationships fail because of this.

"What if I promise that you won't fall in love with me?"

Chapter Ten

PAISLEY

I SNORTED. "You obviously don't know me." I'd fall in love with Ted Bundy if he smiled at me the right way.

"You doubt me?" He held out his arms. "Do you see any women in love with me?"

I laughed because he was gorgeous, and I was sure there was someone somewhere who had a crush on him.

"No, but that doesn't mean they don't exist."

"I'll give you that." He patted me on the leg and stood. "You think about it. I'm here if you need me."

There really wasn't much to think about, except why my plan hadn't worked. Why did he still want to have sex with me? I didn't think I was lousy in bed, but I couldn't be that good either. Otherwise, at least one ex-boyfriend would have fallen in love with me back.

What I really needed was someone to talk to about this situation, but I was hesitant to tell my friends.

Just like that, it was like a lightbulb went off in my head.

I didn't want to tell them because I knew that they would tell me not to sleep with him again. Which meant, deep down, I wanted it to happen again.

I snatched my phone from my purse and sprinted toward my room.

I pulled up the text message thread for the United She-Woman Single Ladies with Our Vibrators So We Never Have Another Bad Date or Experience Romance Again Because Men Suck Club.

> Me: 911. Remember how the guy whose house I'm living in came back last night?

> Me: He's my one-night stand from a month and a half ago.

Pru: What?!

Bree: No way.

> Me: I'm telling the truth.

Elizabeth: I thought his name was CJ. The guy you slept with was something else, right?

> Me: Colin. Colin is his real name. CJ is a family nickname.

Tessa: That sounds very complicated.

They didn't know the half of it.

> Me: It wouldn't be so complicated if he didn't want to sleep with me again.

> Alexis: Holy shit. What are you going to do?

> Pru: You'd better not sleep with him.

There it was. The text I needed.
I breathed a sigh of relief.

> Alexis: Why not?

> Pru: Hello?! This is Paisley we're talking about. She can't sleep with him.

> Alexis: I say go for it. You already walked away once, proving to yourself that you can do it.

I reread the last message. *Did Alexis forget who I was?*

> Me: This is different than last time. He was staying in a hotel, so I assumed he didn't live here and was leaving town. But now, he lives here and with me. I can't just walk away.

Alexis: Except he's your brother-in-law's brother. There's more at risk if you fall in love, and I think you're smart enough to know that. Also, he seems like the perfect practice subject. If you can sleep with this guy and not fall for him, maybe you can get out there and find someone in the future.

Pru: Paisley, don't listen to her. This is a bad decision.

Alexis: Let's vote on it.

Tessa: I see Alexis's point, but I'm going to have to agree with Pru. This could end badly.

Bree: I say go for it.

Pru: Traitor. You wouldn't have said that six months ago.

Bree: LOL.

So far, it was two and two.

Crap. Am I really considering letting this vote decide what happens?

Isabelle: Hey. I just saw the texts, but I'm caught up, and I'm also with Alexis. I think Colin would be a good practice "boyfriend."

The next message Isabelle sent was an eggplant and a tulip emoji.

> Elizabeth: I disagree. I think Paisley should wait to fall in love and then have sex with someone. Then, she'll know her feelings are real.

I wrinkled my nose.

> Me: Do you hate me that much? You know how much I love sex.

> Elizabeth: LOL. I don't hate you. I love you, and I'm looking out for you.

> Alexis: It looks like it's three to three. What are you going to do, Paisley? You're the tiebreaker.

> Me: I messaged you all to tell me that I was crazy for even considering it. And now, three of you are telling me to go for it.

> Bree: Whoops.

> Me: Yeah, whoops.

> Alexis: Sleep on it. You don't have to decide today.

That was actually really good advice, except I had wanted her to talk me out of it.

Me: Thanks, ladies. I need to take a mental break after this conversation.

Isabelle: LOL.

Alexis: Understandable, but I have one question before you go.

Me: What's that?

Alexis: Is he as hot as you remembered?

I smiled and shook my head. For a bunch of man-haters, we sure liked the male species.

Me: No.

Alexis: Boo.

Me: He's hotter.

Alexis: LOL. So, are you going to go for it or not?

Me: I have no freaking clue what I'm going to do.

I turned off the screen and dropped my phone on my bed. I thought about our messages as I changed out of my work clothes and headed to the kitchen to find something to eat. I still didn't know what I should do.

A delicious smell hit me halfway there, and suddenly, my mind was solely on food.

Colin was at the stove, cooking something when I got there.

"That smells so good."

He looked over his shoulder and smiled at me. "Thanks."

I moved closer to get a peek at what he was eating. "Would you happen to be making enough to share?"

"Nope."

My jaw dropped open. I couldn't believe he'd been so rude.

He looked at me and licked his bottom lip. "Told you I could keep you from falling in love with me."

Chapter Eleven

PAISLEY

DESPITE COLIN'S little stunt with telling me I couldn't have any of his food, he had shared with me that night, and we'd decided to take turns cooking the rest of the week.

It was Friday, so technically, it was his night to make dinner, but it was also the weekend, so I wasn't going to hold him to it. And by the time I left work, I was fantasizing about pizza, sweatpants, and a good movie.

I'd promised my dad I would stop by on my way home to help him with his computer. I was not that computer savvy, but my father made me look like an IT whiz.

"Hey, Dad," I called out and closed the front door behind me.

My mom came around the corner first. "Hey, honey. What are you doing here?"

"I told Dad I would help him with his computer."

"Oh."

"Oh what?"

"He's not here. He went golfing this afternoon."

I wasn't surprised. He loved to golf almost as much as he loved my mother.

"It's fine," I told my mom. "Dad already told me what was wrong when we talked earlier today."

I headed to the office upstairs, where I found a sticky note on the monitor, telling me *thanks*.

"I haven't even fixed it yet," I said out loud even though I was the only one in the room.

Smiling, I sat down and went on a hunt to see if I could figure out the problem.

It took me less than five minutes to solve. Shaking my head but grinning, I wrote *You're welcome* on the notepad, pulled it off, and stuck it next to my dad's note.

I went in search of my mom to tell her I'd fixed the computer problem and found her in her bedroom, going through her clothes in her walk-in closet.

"Hey, Mom. I got it done."

"Oh good." She hung up the shirt she had been holding and turned to me. "Did you want to stay for dinner?"

"What are you having?" I had to ask because my mother was an excellent cook.

"I think your dad is going to make some burgers on the grill. It's getting colder out, and he wants to grill one last time before winter gets here."

It sounded good but not as good as pizza.

"I think I'll pass. Thank you though."

"Suit yourself." My mom pointed to a shelf to my right. "Can you hand me the box there?"

"Sure."

"So, your sister told me that Felix's brother came home early. How is that going?"

Well, Mom, it's kind of complicated. See, Colin and I had amazing sex before we knew that our siblings were married. And now, he wants to sleep with me again. And I want that, too, but I'm not sure I can keep my heart and my vagina separate.

"It's going fine. He's a good roommate, and he's kind enough to let me stay at his house until I find a place of my own."

My mother eyed me the way only mothers could. "You're sure? Audrey said you got up and went to your room in the middle of dinner."

I silently cursed my sister. She didn't have to tell our mom *everything*.

"I went to bed early for unrelated reasons," I lied and hoped that her supermom radar wouldn't catch me.

"Good. I worry about you, you know. You can always live here."

I smiled. "I know, and I thank you. But I am looking forward to having my own place again."

"Are you still thinking about buying?"

"Yes. I found a fixer-upper that will be really cute once it's done."

My mom's eyebrows flew up. "You want to buy a house that needs work?"

"Why are you looking at me like that?"

"Because you've never done anything like that before. HGTV makes that stuff look easier than it is."

"I know."

"And instead of hiring someone to do renovations that money might be better spent on a house that doesn't need work."

"I know."

"Do you have a realtor yet?"

"No."

"You'd better find one; otherwise, it doesn't matter how many houses you see online if you're not going to look at them in person."

"I know."

And this was why I didn't want to live with my parents. I knew my mother was right, but I didn't like to be made to feel like I was a kid again and needed their advice for everything.

"I'm going realtor-shopping this weekend." I hadn't really been planning on it, but I sure made it sound that way.

My mother smiled. "Oh good."

"On that note, I'm going to head home."

"You're not leaving because of me, are you?"

I chuckled. "No. Just have stuff to do before I go to bed tonight."

"I understand that. This closet isn't going to rearrange itself."

I gave my mom a hug. "I'll see you later. Tell Dad I said hi and that I'm sorry I missed him."

"Will do."

I let myself out of the house, and as soon as I got to my car, I called up my favorite pizza restaurant to order delivery. Since it was Friday, I was sure they were busy, and I was hoping to be sitting in front of my couch with food in my hand in less than an hour.

When I pulled into the driveway, I noticed an unfamiliar car but didn't think much of it until I walked inside and saw a strange man sitting on the couch.

"Hello," I said.

He grinned and stood. "Hey, you must be Paisley." He came toward me with his hand out. "I'm Mateo, Colin's friend."

"Where is Colin?" I asked as I shook Mateo's hand.

"He's getting ready."

Mateo had the most beautiful brown eyes I'd ever seen with eyelashes that women paid a lot of money for.

"I'm jealous of your eyes," I blurted out.

Mateo laughed, and a voice behind him said, "No falling in love with my friend, Paisley."

Mateo stepped out of the way to reveal Colin standing in the living room in dark jeans that fit him superbly and a button-up shirt that was completely open, revealing his muscular chest and abs.

Thankfully, he was messing with his cuff, so he missed me gawking at him, but his friend saw. When I glanced his way, Mateo winked at me.

"What are you guys up to tonight?"

I had just told my mom I wanted to be alone, but now

that it looked like Colin had plans, I was disappointed he wouldn't be at home tonight.

Colin looked up as he rolled up his sleeve. "We're going to meet up with some friends I haven't seen in months."

"Yeah, since Colin won't let me have a party here, I have to bring him to people."

Colin sighed. "I didn't say you couldn't. I just asked you to wait a couple weeks."

"Right. That's code for *it's never going to happen*."

Colin rolled his eyes as he buttoned up his shirt, and I mourned the loss of his sexy body.

I must have made a noise because both men looked at me in concern.

"You okay?" Colin asked.

"Yeah, I'm fine." *Just horny, thanks to you.*

"What are you doing tonight?"

Ten years ago, I would have been embarrassed to admit I was staying home while others were going out for the night, but I was inching toward thirty, so I didn't care so much anymore if people didn't think I was cool.

"I'm staying in tonight with a movie and pizza."

Colin looked at his friend. "I like her plan better."

"Don't even think about it," Mateo said. "We're going to have fun."

I smiled at the two of them. "If you'll excuse me, I need to go change out of my work clothes." *And maybe have some fun with my vibrator again.* "I hope you have a good night," I said and quickly headed to my room.

Chapter Twelve

COLIN

"SO, THAT'S PAISLEY?" Mateo asked with a smirk on his face. "She's pretty."

I sighed as he started his car. "If you're going to be an ass, I'm staying home." I should have never told Mateo about my first encounter with Paisley.

"I can't believe you'd say that to me." And now, he had the audacity to act offended. "All I said was that she was pretty."

"I've known you too long. What you really meant was, *I'd bone her*, or, *Way to go, man*."

Mateo burst out laughing. "I admit, I might have said something like that way back in high school or even college, but I'm not going to nowadays."

"I appreciate that."

Mateo put the car in drive. "Seriously though, good job," he said and hit the gas.

"Asshole," I muttered.

———

"You have been nursing that beer for the last hour and a half."

I glared at Scotty for opening his big mouth because I'd already known that.

"What the hell, Colin? Why are you being so slow?" Mateo asked.

Because I didn't want to get super drunk tonight. "I'm not being slow. I'm simply taking my time."

Leann snorted. "Same thing."

I raised my beer and drank what was left. "Man, I sure missed you all," I said sarcastically.

The group laughed. I'd wanted them to be offended.

"You haven't seen us in a long time," Scotty said. "You're supposed to drink up."

"I didn't drink a lot in England. I don't have the same tolerance I had before."

"Bullshit," Leann said, coughing into her fist, but her attention was dragged away by something else. She stood and waved. "Clarice, Janie," she yelled.

Two women turned in our direction and started for our table.

Mateo leaned close to me and lowered his voice. "Hey, man, you know I'm just giving you crap. If you don't want to be out tonight, I won't hold it against you if you go home."

I felt bad because I hadn't been that excited about coming out. It was my first full weekend back, and I had things I needed to do now that I was home. But I could see how much Mateo wanted to spend time with me, and my to-do list could wait.

"Nah, I want to be here."

He grinned. "That's what I like to hear." He tilted his head toward Leann and the two women. "Leann invited a couple friends tonight. I heard they're both single."

"That's nice."

"That's nice?" He shook his head, his face full of disappointment. "I want you to remember that you said you wanted to be here."

"Huh?"

Mateo backed away, and in a loud voice, he said, "I challenge you to match me drink for drink tonight, Colin."

The guy was nuts. There was no way I could do that.

But before I could say no, he said, "I noticed your new roomie admiring my eyes. So, how about this? If you can't keep up with me, I'm going to ask Paisley out."

Oh shit. I couldn't let that happen. Not only because I wanted Paisley for myself, but also because I couldn't let her fall in love with Mateo. He would only break her heart.

I gritted my teeth and narrowed my eyes. "You're on."

———

I was drunk.

If I closed my eyes now, the room would spin.

But I didn't know if I could keep up much longer. I could tell Mateo was intoxicated, too, but he was probably feeling better than me.

"Hey, handsome."

I turned my head toward the voice to my left. I had to blink a couple of times to get the woman's face in focus.

"Hey..."

"Clarice."

I grinned. "Hey, Clarice."

"You're shitfaced, aren't you?"

"Totally."

She laughed. "When Leann told me she had some single friends, I didn't think they'd be so hot. But I also didn't know they'd be this drunk."

I pointed to myself. "*Moi?*"

"Yeah, you."

"I am hot or drunk?"

"Both."

"Sorry. I don't normally get wasted, but I had to do it."

She raised her eyebrows. "You had to do it?"

"Yeah. Mateo said he was going to ask out my roommate if I didn't keep up with him."

She looked confused, and because of the alcohol, it took me a few seconds to realize that she was wondering if my roommate was a man.

"My roommate is a she."

She smiled. "Oh, okay. I was wondering why Leann would tell me she had single friends if they didn't bat for my team."

I started laughing.

"Dude, I'm not that funny."

"Sorry."

"So, why can't Mateo date your roommate?"

"Because he'll break her heart."

"Aww...that's so sweet of you to look out for her."

"And because she's mine."

"That makes more sense." She gave me a side-eye. "You know she doesn't belong to anyone, right?"

"I know." *Duh.* "Besides, she doesn't want to sleep with me again anyway."

"Poor you."

I narrowed my eyes. "I don't think you mean that."

"I don't. I'm sure you have plenty of women to sleep with."

"But I want her."

"And that's my cue."

"Your cue to what?"

"It was nice to meet you, Colin." Clarice scooted out of the booth and walked up to Leann. The two talked for about half a minute before Leann came over.

"Okay, Colin and Mateo, I am cutting you off."

"Why?" Mateo whined from across the table.

"I don't need you killing Colin with alcohol poisoning."

Mateo looked at me. "You're fine, right?"

I scoffed. "I'm fine."

"And I'm the Pope. No more drinks for either of you."

I grinned at Mateo. "I drank everything you did. That means, I win. No asking Paisley out."

"Oh no," Mateo said, but he didn't sound that disappointed.

Chapter Thirteen

PAISLEY

IT WAS AFTER MIDNIGHT, and I was thinking about going to bed soon. I had less than fifteen minutes left on my movie when it sounded like someone was at the front door. I heard the jingling of keys, and a couple seconds later, there was a knock.

When I got to the door, I flipped on the front light to see who was outside in hopes that it was Colin and not a stranger.

It was both.

Colin had his arm around a very pretty woman who I didn't recognize. My mind raced with what he was doing with her.

Was he bringing her home to have sex with her, and was he doing that because I wouldn't have sex with him?

It crossed my mind that it was my fault, but then I immediately corrected my inner voice and reminded myself I didn't want someone who was going to go out and sleep with the first person he'd met, so maybe I had lucked out.

I unlocked the door and swung it open.

"Thank God," the woman said.

She walked into the house, practically dragging Colin with her. I now saw that he had his arm around her, so he didn't fall over.

The woman shoved a set of keys in my hand. "Here. He couldn't figure out how to unlock it. I hope I didn't wake you."

I pointed to the TV. "No, I was still awake."

The woman led Colin over to the couch and dropped him on his back.

He groaned and blinked up at the ceiling but didn't say anything else.

"Is he okay?" I asked.

"Just really drunk."

"Oh." I hadn't expected Colin to drink so much that he was almost unconscious.

"Mateo told Colin that if he didn't match him drink for drink, he was going to ask out someone named Paisley."

I gasped. "I'm Paisley."

The woman smiled. "Hi, Paisley. I'm Leann."

I wanted to ask more about the drinking match between Colin and Mateo, but I didn't want to sound desperate. "Nice to meet you." I looked down at my drunk roommate. "I guess."

Leann chuckled. "Yeah, it could be under better

circumstances." She leaned down and patted Colin's knee. "And sorry to do this, but he's your problem now."

"My problem?" I asked as Leann walked around the couch to the door.

"Yeah. We have to take a drunk Mateo home too."

Curious who *we* was, I tried to look outside to the driveway through the window next to the door, but I couldn't see anything from the angle where I was standing. "I won't keep you."

"Good luck with Colin. He must really like you if he's willing to try to outdrink Mateo."

I didn't get a chance to respond because Leann was out the door before I could form a word.

I locked it and shut off the light before wandering over to Colin. His eyes were closed, and his breathing was deep, so I assumed he'd fallen asleep. I considered leaving him where he was, except one foot was on the floor and he still had his shoes on. It looked too uncomfortable, and as it was, he was already going to wake up, feeling bad.

"Colin," I yelled because I knew it was going to take some volume to get him up and moving.

He blinked and slowly looked around before his eyes landed on my face.

"It's time to go to bed."

"Okay." He reached for the back of the couch to help him sit up, but he slipped and fell back.

I grabbed his other arm. "Let me help you."

Together, we got him up to a sitting position.

"Do you want to take your shoes off?"

"Yeah." He looked down at his feet, but that was it.

I sighed and knelt. "If your feet stink, I'm definitely not sleeping with you." I said it low, but Colin let out one single chuckle, which made me smile.

And surprisingly, his feet weren't that bad.

"Okay, tiger," I said as I stood, "let's get you up and to your bedroom."

Getting him standing took a little more work, and he had to put his arm around me like he had with Leann, so I could get him to his room, but we made it. I started for his bed once we reached the doorway, but he didn't walk with me.

"What?" I asked.

"Teeth."

"Teeth?"

"Yeah. I need to brush them." He bared them to me, as if that proved he needed to clean them.

"I'm not brushing your teeth."

I walked toward his bed again, and Colin stood his ground.

"Fine. I will help you, but I'm not doing it for you."

We walked to his en suite bathroom, and I propped his ass against the counter in the corner in hopes that the sink and the wall would keep him upright.

I found his toothbrush and toothpaste, got it ready, and handed it to him.

He brushed his teeth about as well as a kid did, but I supposed it was better than nothing.

"Can we go to bed now, or do you need to pee?"

I meant it as a joke, but then he nodded his head, and he didn't even wait for me to turn around before he unbuttoned his jeans.

I quickly helped him over to the toilet, so he didn't fall and so I wouldn't have to see him pull out his penis. As he went to the bathroom, I tried to think of anything else but what I was currently doing.

"Done," he announced. The toilet seat closed with a boom as he flushed. He laughed. "Whoops. I dropped it."

Thankfully, Colin steered himself toward the sink to wash his hands. In the mirror, I saw that he hadn't buttoned his jeans back up, and I had to look away before I stared too intently at his treasure trail.

After his hands were washed and dried, I asked, "Can we go to bed now?"

"Yep."

"Where are your pajamas?" I looked around his room, hoping to see previously worn ones on the bed or on a chair somewhere.

"I don't wear any."

"What?" I spun back to him just in time to see his completely naked backside.

Lord have mercy. I must not have gotten a chance to see this part of him the night we'd had sex because I would have remembered an ass like that.

But thankfully, Colin didn't try to flash me or anything. He immediately got into bed and pulled up the covers.

"Are you going to be okay? Do you need a bucket or

anything?" I held up a finger. "Actually, hold on. I'll be right back."

I went and found the biggest water bottle he had in his cupboard and filled it up before grabbing a bottle of ibuprofen. I brought them to his room and set them on the nightstand.

"This is for when you wake up, feeling like shit."

Colin picked up my hand. "Thank you."

"You're welcome." I squeezed his fingers. "Need anything else?"

"Just to be inside you again."

Whoa. I had *not* expected that.

"I think about our night together all the time. And I dream about your pussy almost every night."

I was speechless. What did I say back? The guy was drunk, so I shouldn't encourage him, but I didn't want to sound rude.

A soft snore floated up from the bed.

And he was asleep.

I untangled my hand from his and left his room. I went back and turned off the television and shut off all the lights, but even while I did those things, my mind was somewhere else.

I couldn't believe he still thought about me that way.

Chapter Fourteen

COLIN

MY HEAD FELT like someone was performing brain surgery on me without anesthesia. I hadn't had a hangover like this since college.

I slowly rolled to my side and saw that someone had left me water and pain medicine. I didn't know who it was, but I was very thankful.

The last thing I remembered from the night before was throwing back a shot with Mateo and him saying something about getting another round of beers. After that, my memory was incredibly fuzzy.

After carefully sitting up, I took the pills left for me and drank as much water as I could before my stomach started to protest. When I pulled back my comforter, I noticed I was naked. I hoped that even though someone had left me the medicine and water, they hadn't helped me get to bed.

I put on a pair of sweatpants and a sweatshirt and forced myself out of my room.

I found Paisley at the kitchen table in front of her laptop. She looked up when she heard me.

"Wow, I didn't expect you to be up for another hour or so."

"Do I look as bad as I feel?" I asked, taking the seat adjacent to her.

She smiled sympathetically. "Let's just say, I'm glad I stayed home last night."

"I never should have drunk that much."

She looked up from her computer. "Why did you?"

Ooh. I couldn't tell her Mateo was going to ask her out if I didn't.

"Mateo challenged me." She just didn't need to know why he'd challenged me.

"Hmm."

I couldn't tell if her sound was judgmental or not, so I moved on. "How did I get home?"

"Leann brought you inside, but it sounded like there were others in the car, waiting for her."

"She helped me inside? Did she help me to bed too?"

"Oh, no, that was all me."

I winced, remembering my nakedness when I woke up. "Did I make it hard on you?"

"You made me help you brush your teeth. And you peed while I was in the bathroom."

"I'm sorry."

"To be fair, I stayed because I was afraid you'd fall over."

"Damn, I was really drunk."

"Yes. Yes, you were. Do you remember saying anything to me last night?"

I tried hard to conjure up anything after the bar, but it was like a blank wall. "No. Shit. Did I say something bad? Or inappropriate?"

Paisley looked down to the other side of her computer. "Sorry, I need to answer this." Her expression was a little too serious.

Figuring she was referring to a phone call, I was surprised when she started typing on her cell.

After she finished, I thought she would respond to my question, but either she'd forgotten or she was trying to avoid answering.

"Everything okay?"

"Yeah. Just trying to find a realtor. My friend just bought a house, so I asked for hers, but the person who'd helped her is having surgery, so they're out of commission for a couple of months."

This had me sitting up straight. "A realtor? Are you going to look at the house you told me about before? I can still help with it if you need me to."

I was really hoping I'd get to spend some time with her.

"No, it sold."

That wasn't good.

"Maybe you can find another like it," I suggested.

"I don't know about that anymore."

I started to panic. What if she didn't want my help anymore?

"I talked to my mom yesterday, and she pointed out that I don't know anything about home renovations besides what I've seen on TV."

"But I told you I would help."

She chuckled. "More like do it all. I would be the one helping you. That's not fair, and I just can't ask that of you. It's not reasonable. We barely know each other."

"I wouldn't say barely," I mumbled.

"You know what I mean."

"Yeah," I reluctantly agreed.

"I think the best thing to do is find a smaller home that doesn't need work." She smiled at me. "That will just get me out of your house that much faster."

But I didn't want her out of my house.

I needed to think fast if I was going to keep her around and spend time with her. Too bad for me, it was really hard to think with a hangover.

"Ooh...I like her."

I looked over at Paisley. I'd been so lost in my own head that I didn't notice she'd moved on from our conversation.

"Like who?" I asked.

"This realtor. She looks about my age, and she's a redhead, just like me. Her name is Sloan Stanton. Oh, I love the name Sloan."

"That's exactly how I picked my last realtor," I said a little too harshly.

"Well, it's a good thing she also has a four-point-five rating out of five stars." She gave me a pointed look. "Unless you have someone better in mind?"

A lightbulb went off in my head.

"I take it by the look on your face, you do?" she asked.

It had previously crossed my mind that I could ask someone to only show Paisley the worst places to live so she wouldn't want to move, but that was too mean and sneaky. But it had gotten me thinking about something else.

"Actually, I don't. The realtor I used when I bought this place wasn't that great, but I didn't want to take the time to start over. Plus, as an architect, I knew what I was looking for." I smiled. "And that's why you should take me with you when you go house-hunting."

She gave me a deadpan look. "You want to look at houses with me?"

"Why not? It will be fun."

She looked at me like I was a stranger.

"What? You don't think it's fun?"

"Maybe the first couple, but it gets old fast."

"I disagree, which means I'm the right person to take with you."

She wrinkled her nose. "Would it be weird that I take you instead of one of my friends?"

"You can take them too. Besides, I'm your roommate. I'm going to know you better than they do very soon."

Her eyebrows shot up.

"Contact this realtor lady and let me know when you need me."

"Okay." She picked up her phone and punched in some numbers before lifting it to her ear. "Hi. Yes, my name is Paisley, and I'm in the market for a home. I was wondering if you'd have time to fit me into your schedule."

Pause.

She grinned. "Great. And you have time today? Wonderful. I would love to see as many houses as you can show me today. Five to ten? Wow. That's amazing."

When she'd said she was going to start house-shopping, I hadn't thought it would be today. I felt like shit, and there was a chance that riding around in a car might cause me to throw up.

"Can you hold on a moment, please?" Paisley pulled the phone away from her face. "Are you okay, Colin? You look a little pale."

"I..."

She flashed her dark screen at me. "Gotcha. I'm not going to look at five houses today."

Relief poured through my body. "What did you do that for?" I complained.

"It's revenge for when you told me I couldn't eat any of your food."

I smiled. "Okay, I deserved that."

"You kind of did."

"On that note, I think it's time for me to park my butt in front of the TV."

"Should we watch some *Charmed?*"

"Let's."

Her mouth dropped open. "I was joking."

"I'm not. Let's do it."

Chapter Fifteen

PAISLEY

I LOOKED at my phone and tapped Colin on the shoulder from where he had his head on a pillow, propped on my lap. "I need to get up."

He looked over his shoulder at me. "What? Why? The show is getting good."

I laughed. I was glad he liked my favorite show, but I had plans that night. "I have to get ready. I'm meeting up with some friends tonight."

He sat up and looked at me. "We had our nights crossed, huh?"

"Yeah, but unlike you, I'm not going to get really drunk, and you won't have to put me to bed."

He winced. "What are you doing?"

"Going for dinner and drinks. Nothing exciting." I glanced at the television. "You can keep watching the show without me. I've seen them all plenty of times. You don't have to wait for me."

"Thanks," he said, but he sounded disappointed.

By his lack of enthusiasm, I figured Colin would be watching something else when I left an hour later, but he was still going strong with *Charmed*. I was glad I hadn't packed the DVDs away in my storage unit.

"Have fun tonight," I said to him.

He smiled wistfully at me. "You too."

———

When I got to the bar and grill, Isabelle and Elizabeth were already there.

"Hey," I said as I slid into my seat at our table. "You haven't been here long, have you? I thought I was right on time."

"You are," Elizabeth said. "We just got here too."

"So, how was everyone's week?" I asked after our server brought us our drinks and took our food order.

"Fine," Isabelle said. "But I want to know how your week was. You never told us what you decided. Did you sleep with Colin again?"

"No. It's pretty tempting"—*especially after his confession last night*—"but no, I haven't."

Elizabeth and Isabelle stared at me.

"What?"

Isabelle shook her head. "I'm shocked, is all."

"Same," Elizabeth admitted.

"Thanks," I said sarcastically.

Isabelle's eyes filled with concern. "Come on, Paisley.

We didn't mean it as an insult," she said. "We love that you love so much. It's what makes you, you."

"I suppose," I said.

"I'm serious. Right, Elizabeth?"

Elizabeth nodded. "One hundred percent."

"Then, why is everyone telling me to not sleep with men?"

"Because we don't like to see you get hurt," Elizabeth said. "And we want you to be treated the way you deserve to be treated."

They did have a good point.

"But I have to say, I'm proud of you, Paisley," Elizabeth continued. "And forget what I said the other day. I think you should go for it. Make Colin your practice guy."

Now, I was the one who was stunned.

"For real?" Isabelle took the words right out of my mouth.

"Why the sudden change of heart?" I asked.

"You've already shown progress with this guy." Elizabeth took a sip of her wine. "You had a one-night stand with him and didn't get his phone number. And even though you're living with him, you haven't slept with him again. The more I think about it, the more I'm wondering if this guy is special in that you're not treating him like everyone else. I think if you're going to find someone to practice not falling in love with, he's it."

Isabelle raised her eyebrows. "You don't think living together will add complications?"

I looked back and forth between my friends. "I'm so confused. You two are both switching sides?"

Isabelle shook her finger back and forth. "Oh, no, I'm not changing my mind. I still think you should go for it. I'm just playing devil's advocate with Elizabeth."

"Yeah, and my love life," I pointed out.

My friends laughed.

"Oh, relax. I just wanted to see if Elizabeth really felt like you should give it a shot with Colin."

"I do really feel that way. I think sometimes, people need to try to do things outside their comfort zone if they're going to find out what they like and to learn more about themselves."

When Elizabeth said this, she looked right at Isabelle, who didn't seem to notice.

I wanted to ask more, but Isabelle grinned at me. "You heard the woman."

"Yes, I did."

"So...are you going to go for it?" Isabelle asked.

———

I got home around ten and was surprised to see Colin still awake, watching TV. Although it looked like he had given up on *Charmed*.

"I thought you'd be in bed," I told him.

"It's not that late."

"But you were very hungover this morning. I figured you would need the extra rest."

And I really had been counting on him to be in bed already. It would have given me an excuse to delay the conversation I was about to have with him.

"If I didn't know any better, I would say, you're disappointed."

"No, not at all."

"Did dinner go okay?"

"Yeah, it was nice."

Colin raised his brow. "Did you want to sit down and stay awhile, or are you leaving again?"

I chuckled nervously. The weather was cold after the sun went down, and I still had my coat and shoes on. I removed my jacket and kicked off my kitten heels, but I didn't sit.

"I wanted to talk to you about something."

"Oh? And what would that be? Are you going to tell me what I said to you last night?"

That was a no. I was not repeating the words he'd said to me.

"No. I wanted to talk to you about sex."

"In general or with you and me?"

"You and me."

"Did you change your mind?" He groaned as his eyes filled with heat. "Please tell me I get to be inside you again."

"Yes." I held up my hand. "But I have a few rules first."

"I accept."

"What?"

"Whatever your rules are, yes. I'll do it."

I laughed. "I appreciate that, but can I tell you what they are first?"

"We're only wasting time, but sure. Hit me with the rules."

I pulled my phone out of my purse and pulled up my Notes app, where Isabelle, Elizabeth, and I had come up with rules to help me not fall in love.

I cleared my throat. "*Number one...*" I said, starting at the top of the list.

1. *No sleeping in the same bed together. We have sex, and then the other goes back to his or her bed.*
2. *No dates.*
3. *No pet names.*
4. *No being boyfriend-y. No buying me gifts or texting to ask how my day is.*
5. *You have to keep your promise about helping me not fall in love with you.*
6. *No kissing.*
7. *We can have sex only four times a week.*

"Hold on. I'm going to cut you off there. Four times a week? That's it?" He shook his head. "Nope. That doesn't work for me."

"You already said yes to everything."

"Well, I change my mind. Now, I'm saying no."

I gave him the side-eye. "So, you would rather not have sex at all than have sex only four times a week?"

He leaned back and put his arms on the back of the couch. "Yep. I want to be able to have sex with you whenever I want—with you willing, of course—and I don't want to be worrying about if we already had sex four times that week. Nope. Too hard."

I rubbed my thighs together. It was incredibly sexy that he wanted me that much. And even though he'd called my bluff, I was going to give in. My friends and I had prepared for this anyway.

"Okay then, once a day. That's more than four times a week."

He rubbed the stubble on his chin. "Once a day during the week and twice on the weekend."

I supposed we would have more time together on the weekend. "Okay. You got yourself a deal."

"And oral sex doesn't count. If you want to ride my face and then my dick, I don't want to have to wait a day. Fuck that."

Oh God. Now, I was picturing doing just that.

Colin snapped his finger, and I looked up to see a glint in his eyes.

"Is there anything else on your list?"

I checked even though I knew that was it. "No."

"Do we have a deal then?"

Moment of truth.

I took a deep breath and said..."Yes."

Colin jumped off the couch and came toward me.

Chapter Sixteen

PAISLEY

COLIN THREW me over his shoulder and sprinted down the hall and into his bedroom.

"We're going to have sex now?"

"I've been waiting almost two months for this. I'm not waiting a second more." He bent over and dropped me on his bed.

"Smells good."

He grinned. "I washed my sheets while you were gone."

"Just for me?"

"I didn't know that this was going to happen, but let's go with yes."

I watched as Colin yanked off his sweatshirt and kicked off his pants. No underwear for this guy. He was naked and hard, and I wanted to touch, remembering how good he'd tasted.

I reached out for his dick, but he swatted my hand away.

"Oh, no. You don't get to touch until I say I'm ready."

Pushing my bottom lip out in a pout, I asked, "Why not?"

He walked over to his nightstand. As he rummaged around, he asked, "When you say sex once a day, what qualifies as once?"

Good question. Isabelle, Elizabeth, and I hadn't discussed that part.

"After you have an orgasm, I guess."

"That's what I figured." He dropped a single condom on the bed. "But it has to be an orgasm when I'm inside your pussy, seeing as how oral doesn't count." He attacked my clothes, getting them off me within seconds. "Also, an orgasm by hand doesn't count either," he said as he slid his fingers between my legs and rubbed my clit.

I gasped and rotated my hips over his hand. But all too soon, he took it away.

Tilting his chin up, he said, "Move toward the headboard."

I quickly did as he'd said and watched as he climbed onto the bed and lay down on his stomach.

"Open those legs wide for me. I didn't get to taste you last time, and I've been regretting it since I woke up the next morning." He looked up into my eyes. "Of course, I didn't know I was going to wake up alone either."

I bit my lip. "I'm sorry. But I explained why I had to do

it." Letting my legs fall open, I asked, "How's this for an apology?"

I was half-joking since I was the one who was going to get head, but Colin seemed to think it was sincere.

"It's a good start." He kissed the top of my cleft. "It's a real good start."

I couldn't agree more.

"So, tell me, Paisley, what do you like?" He blew on my clit. "Do you like to be teased?" He planted a peck there. "Do you like to be kissed?" He circled his tongue around it next. "Do you like to be licked?" Following that, he sucked it between his lips. "Or do you like full pressure?"

I moaned and thrashed my head. "I like it all."

He rolled us over. "Or how about the *riding my face* thing? You liked when I brought that up earlier."

I gasped. "How did you know?"

"You zoned out on me." He squeezed my ass. "Remember how you let me fuck your face?"

I nodded.

"I want you to fuck mine now. Tell me what you want. Tell me what you need."

When I hesitated, he slapped my butt. "Ride my face, Paisley."

Grabbing on to the headboard, I lowered my pussy toward Colin's mouth. He kissed the inside of my thigh and dragged his lips up to my core.

As his tongue darted out and licked my center, he wrapped his hands around my thighs and held me close to him.

Even though I was on top and could move as I pleased, Colin was in control. He started with a little teasing.

"Please, I need more."

He moved to kissing and licking, and by the time he sucked my little nub into his mouth, I exploded. I clung to the headboard but was unable to stay upright, and I fell onto the bed, half curled into a ball.

Colin got up on one elbow, leaned over, and kissed me.

He pulled back abruptly. "Oops. You said no kissing. Sorry."

"I did?" I honestly couldn't remember.

He nodded.

I shrugged a shoulder. "We already kissed the night we met. I think it's okay to keep doing that." I snagged him around the neck and pulled him back down.

We spent a good ten minutes kissing and touching each other all over. Colin flicked my nipples and caressed my back. I cupped his beautiful butt and ran my fingers over his chest. As we played, I slowly uncurled my body to lay fully underneath him, and when I did, I took his hard length in my hand.

We both groaned, but he gently pulled my hand away.

"If you keep doing that, I won't last very long inside you, and we can't have that."

He grabbed the condom he'd dropped on the bed earlier, ripped it open, and quickly put it on. He pulled me into his arms. "I think I'm the luckiest bastard in the world," he said and slowly pushed his cock inside me.

By the time he reached the hilt, I came again.

"I was wrong. I *am* the luckiest bastard."

———

Colin took a heel and dragged me to the end of the bed.

"I—I can't anymore."

He had given me so many orgasms, one after the other, but he hadn't come once yet. And I was pretty sure that if I came again, I would die.

"It's okay, Paisley. This time is for me."

I waited for him to push into me again, but he ripped off the condom and stroked his dick over my pussy without going inside.

His penis looked swollen and almost painful, and I realized how long he'd held off so that he could pleasure me repeatedly.

I licked my palm and put it on the outside of his cock. He groaned in the back of his throat as I applied pressure, and I watched in fascination as we brought him to climax.

His seed burst out of him and all over my stomach, and Colin's chest heaved in and out with deep breaths. "Holy shit, I didn't last long."

I threw my head back and laughed. I knew he was talking about the last few minutes, but he had to give himself credit for the whole thing. "You lasted longer than any guy I've ever been with."

He kissed me. "I hope you remember that for a long, long-ass time." He stepped away. "Let me get you a towel."

Rather than dropping my feet to the floor, I moved up

on the bed until he came back. "Hey, you didn't come inside me."

"Don't worry. I'm totally spent and ready for bed."

"Oh, thank God," I muttered and closed my eyes while I waited.

A hand slapped my ass, and my head flew off the bed as I was startled awake.

I looked around, and it took me a few seconds to realize I was curled up with Colin's pillow, lying on my stomach in his bed.

"Sleeping beauty, it's time to go to your own room," Colin said from beside me.

I remembered being half awake when Colin had come back and cleaned my stomach off, but when I'd gotten under the covers, I had no idea.

I groaned out of frustration. "But your bed is so warm."

"Your rules, remember?"

"Fuck my rules." Sleeping was way more important.

I laid my head back down, only to have the covers ripped off me a second later.

Colin picked me up in his arms, carried me across the hall, and dropped me down in my own bed before I could process what was happening.

"You're a butthole," I yelled toward the hall.

"Just making sure you don't fall in love with me," he called back.

I couldn't help the smile that spread across my face as I slipped under my own covers and pulled them to my chin.

Chapter Seventeen

COLIN

SUNDAY MORNING STARTED out a hundred times better than the day before. I woke up, refreshed, without a hangover, and so sexually satisfied that my dick wasn't even sporting morning wood.

Remembering Paisley naked and underneath me did have that changing quickly, but I was still feeling good.

After getting out of bed, I found Paisley's clothes on my floor, so I picked them up and started folding them until I remembered the rules. I was supposed to make sure she didn't fall in love with me.

This put me in a tough situation because I didn't want her to hate me either. I didn't know where this relationship —if it could be called that—was going. I didn't know if I even wanted her to fall in love with me someday because I wasn't in love with her—yet. But if there was a chance for us, I didn't want to blow it by being too mean.

In the end, I had promised her I wouldn't do anything

boyfriend-like, and I wasn't going to break my promise of adhering to her guidelines. And who knew? Maybe doing just that would be the way to her heart.

I picked up her clothes and dumped them on the floor outside her bedroom door. Feeling satisfied with my decision, I went to find breakfast.

———

About an hour later, I heard, "Woohoo," come from Paisley's room, followed by the sound of feet hitting the floor and her door being yanked opened. I didn't know what I expected next, but it wasn't the loud boom as something hit the wall, and, "Motherfucker," was yelled.

Paisley marched out to the living room, where I was sitting on the couch, and glared at me.

"Everything okay?" I asked.

"I just tripped on my pants and ran into the wall."

"Oops."

"*Oops?* That's all you have to say for yourself?"

I shrugged. "I thought about folding your clothes and gently placing them on the floor, but you made the rules, not me, and I figured that was something a boyfriend would do."

She gritted her teeth. "You're right, dammit," she admitted.

I smiled. "However, as your sexual partner, I can offer to kiss it and make it better."

Her mouth twitched, and I suspected she was trying not to smile back.

She held up her bent arm. "It was my elbow. Nothing very exciting."

I stood, walked over to her, kissed her elbow, and went into the kitchen for more coffee. "I went and picked up doughnuts this morning, if you want one?"

She followed me. "I thought you just said you weren't going to do anything a boyfriend would do."

I frowned, not following at first. I shook my head when I realized what she was getting at. "I'm not. You're also my roommate, and I would like to think we're at least friends, and I would do that for anyone staying here."

She seemed to consider this for a moment and must have concluded I was right because she opened the box and picked out a doughnut.

I was going to have to remember this because the roommate/friend excuse might come in handy later.

"So, what were you so excited about?" I asked as I poured myself more coffee.

"Oh. I almost forgot." She picked up her phone and unlocked the screen. "The realtor I emailed yesterday responded, and she said she has a few houses she can even show me today if I'm available."

"Great. When are we going?"

"Never."

"But you just said—"

"I'm going to look at houses. You are not coming with me."

I frowned. "Since when?"

"Since last night."

"How does that change anything?" I protested.

She shrugged. "I don't know. It seems like something a boyfriend would do."

"I agreed to do this before we slept together. One thing has nothing to do with the other." I lifted up my free hand. "But if you feel like it goes against your rules, I understand." I pushed myself off the counter I'd been leaning against and headed for the living room. "You have fun. Make lots of notes, so you remember stuff you liked and didn't like."

"Wait."

I stopped but didn't turn around. "Yeah?"

"I guess you can come. If you still want to. It would be good to have another set of eyes."

I grinned. "You let me know what time. I'll go and shower." I stopped again. "Actually, you know what?"

"What?" Paisley asked as I spun around.

I put my cup on the counter, took the doughnut from her hand, and set it next to my mug.

"You're taking a shower with me."

"What?"

"Hey, we get to have sex twice today, and if we're going to be gone for a while, you're getting your goods now," I said as I picked up her hand and led her down the hall to my room.

"My goods?"

"Yeah, your goods."

"I think this is for you, buddy."

I pushed her up against my bathroom door. "Who came more last night? Me or you?"

She stared at my mouth and swallowed. "Me."

I lifted her chin and kissed her. "Just the way I like it."

Chapter Eighteen

PAISLEY

COLIN and I met Sloan outside the first house she had given me the address to. She held out her hand in greeting.

"Hello. You must be Paisley," she said as we shook hands.

"Yes."

"It's nice to meet you."

"You too."

She looked over at Colin. "And are you the husband? Boyfriend?"

"Friend," I jumped in. "He's just a friend."

"And roommate," he said.

"Kind of roommate, kind of landlord."

"I mean, it is my house, but you're not paying rent, so am I a landlord?"

Sloan smiled as her eyes bounced back and forth between us.

"It's my temporary living situation," I clarified. "My old landlord decided to sell the house I was renting."

She chuckled. "You really don't have to explain your situation to me. I'm just here to show you a house."

"Right, right," I said.

"Shall we go?" she asked, pointing over her shoulder.

"Let's do it."

We made our way to the front door, and as Sloan unlocked it, she said, "I went over your desired locations and things you are looking for in a house, and I set up four for us to look at today. But I want you to remember, I might not get everything on your list, but I will try my hardest." She pushed the door open.

"Oh, I know. And I appreciate you helping me," I said and walked into the entryway.

Unfortunately, right away, I knew I didn't care for this home. When Sloan had asked if there was any type of home I didn't like, I had told her I was open to anything. But I wasn't a big fan of split foyers, which was what this house was. But they were a common house style in Minnesota, so I was going to try to keep an open mind.

"Let's start upstairs, shall we?" Sloan said.

I nodded and followed her.

———

The next house we went to was a little one-story home that I thought was very charming. It was in an older neighborhood with big trees and nice-sized yards.

But as soon as Sloan left Colin and me alone to talk about it in private, he said, "Don't buy it."

"What?" I looked around. "Why not? It's adorable."

"Sure, it's small and cute. So small that it only has a one-stall garage."

"So? I'm one person with only one car."

"But what if you don't always live here alone? Then, you're stuck with only one stall. In winter. In Minnesota."

I knew he was dragging out his sentence to prove a point, but it worked. If I got married, I wouldn't want to have to share the garage.

"I'll put it at the bottom of the list."

———

The third home was two stories and had a two-stall garage.

"There's no main-floor bathroom," Colin pointed out when we were alone.

"What?" I had made a quick walk-through. "How did I not notice that?"

"I don't know. Because you were mesmerized by the large kitchen."

I sighed. "It does have a beautiful kitchen." It had been remodeled in the last five years and was the best part about the house. "I think not having a bathroom down here will be okay?"

He looked at me like I was nuts. "You say that now, but it's going to get old."

"I don't know about that."

"Is there anything at my place that you thought wouldn't be a big deal to live with but has become a burden?"

"Yeah." I grinned. "You."

"You're hilarious," he said in a flat tone, obviously meaning the opposite.

"Thank you."

He looked away and rolled his eyes. "Okay, how about your old place?"

When I'd moved in, I hadn't liked that the garage wasn't attached to the house, but I'd figured I could live with it. About six months later, I'd hated it.

"Fine. You make a good point."

"On to the next house?" he asked.

"I guess so."

———

The fourth house on the realtor's list was toward the lower half of my price range, so I was looking forward to seeing it since it was the last one on today's list. But once again, Colin had to wreck it for me.

"There's only two bedrooms and one bathroom."

"I know, but I can really afford this one. I don't need to worry about getting a roommate to help me pay for it, and if I meet someone, I can sell it."

"That's where you might be wrong. This has been on the market for months and hasn't sold. It's hard to find a buyer for such a small place when they can rent something instead."

I huffed out a breath. "You are really ruining this for me."

Colin winced. "You're right, and I apologize. Just because I point these things out doesn't mean you can't buy any of these properties. Nothing is going to be perfect."

"I'll think about it."

"And you're just getting started. These aren't your only options."

The corner of my mouth lifted in a half smile. "Good point."

"Shall we tell Sloan we're leaving?"

"Might as well."

———

My phone beeped in my purse. We'd gotten home some time ago, and all I was doing was mentally going through each home I'd seen today in my head again. I welcomed the distraction from whoever was texting me.

> Bree: My mom wants me to have an engagement party. What do you think? Will I regret it?

> Alexis: She can't bother you about getting married anymore. She should be fine, right?

Bree: *buzzer sound* You would be wrong. She has now started asking me when I'm going to have a BABY!

Bree's mom had bugged her for years about finding a man and settling down, so I could see why Alexis had thought she would leave her daughter alone now. Turned out, Alexis and I were wrong.

The good part was, it made me smile.

Me: Sorry, Bree.

Bree: Thanks. I want to have a party, but I don't want my mother to ruin it.

Me: Have an engagement dinner with family, and later that night, have an engagement party with friends. Have dinner early, kick everyone out or leave the restaurant and go home, and have a fun party later.

Bree: That is a really good idea.

Me: I try.

Bree: Ladies, you know you're all invited, so I will let you know when it's happening as soon as we set a date.

Alexis: Sounds great.

Bree: Oh, Paisley, how did house-hunting go?

Me: Okay.

Bree: Just okay? I'm sorry.

Me: Thanks.

Alexis: You'll find the perfect place. Just give it a little bit.

Bree: I agree. Enjoy your free rent and wait until "the one" comes along.

Me: Thanks, ladies.

There was a knock on my open bedroom door, so I looked up to see Colin.

"You doing okay? You were quiet on the drive home."

I set my phone down. "Yeah. Disappointed, but I'll survive."

"Good. I was thinking maybe some pizza and beer would make you feel better."

I narrowed my eyes at him. That sounded like a boyfriend-girlfriend thing. "I just had pizza on Friday."

"Right. Then, can I interest you in an orgasm?"

That didn't sound half bad.

"Works for me."

Colin sauntered into my room and slammed a condom

down on my nightstand. "I was hoping you'd say that," he said as he jumped on my bed beside me.

"But just so you know, I am going to be hungry soon, so we're not having sex for hours, like we did last night."

"You're no fun."

"And I get to give you head."

"I take back everything I just said." He rolled onto his back. "I've never met a woman who liked to give blow jobs as much as you."

I moved to straddle him. "Then, maybe you've been with the wrong women," I said with more confidence than I truly felt.

He smiled at me. "Maybe I have been."

I snorted. I had a list of men a mile long who would disagree with him.

Chapter Nineteen

PAISLEY

FRIDAY MORNING, I got ready for work, slipped on some heels, and headed to the kitchen to grab a banana and yogurt to eat in my car for breakfast.

As I entered, I heard a catcall whistle, and I spun around to see Colin standing there, eating a bowl of cereal.

"What are you still doing here?" I asked.

He went to work before me and got off before me, so he was usually gone by the time I left.

"What are you doing, wearing that outfit?" He licked his lips. "Damn, you look delicious. Mmm. You are sexy."

My cheeks heated. I had picked out a red blouse to go with a black pencil skirt. I'd thought I looked good, but I hadn't known I looked that good.

"Thank you," I told him.

He finished his cereal, put his bowl in the dishwasher, and wandered over to me. Pulling me into his arms, he said,

"Do you have time for a quickie?" He kissed my neck and nipped at my shoulder.

"How are you horny? We've had sex every night this week."

I'd had no idea when I made the rule about sex once a day that he would actually take me up on it. Maybe I should have stuck to four times a week, except I was loving every minute of it.

He lifted his head. "Paise, I'm always horny when you're around." He tilted his head back and forth. "Mostly. I do get tired and hungry sometimes."

"Speaking of hungry, I need to grab my breakfast and get out of here, so I'm not late."

"So, no sex?"

I laughed. "No sex."

"After work then." He slid his hand up the back of my thigh and fingered my underwear.

I patted my palm on his hard dick. "It's going to have to wait. We both got invited to have dinner at Audrey and Felix's. I plan to go there straight from work."

Colin groaned and stepped away from me. "I forgot about that." He crossed his arms over his chest. "Can't we skip it?"

I smiled. "I doubt it since my parents and your parents are going to be there too." I picked a banana off the bunch sitting on the counter and went to the fridge to grab my yogurt.

"Okay, now, you're just teasing me."

I shut the door and turned around. "What?"

"You bent over like that on purpose to torture me."

He sounded grumpy, and I had to bite my lip to keep from laughing.

"I apologize." I leaned forward and kissed him on the corner of his mouth. "I didn't mean to."

"Apology accepted."

"Thanks for saying I'm sexy."

"You're welcome."

"I have to go. I'll see you at Audrey and Felix's tonight."

"Yeah, yeah." He also grabbed a banana off the counter and headed to the door with me. He opened it and let me walk out first. "It's going to be a long day."

Being a law-abiding driver, I didn't look at my phone as I drove to work. But I could hear my notification sound, so when I got to the office after my commute, I wasn't surprised that I had texts. But I was shocked to see they were from Colin.

I opened my messages as I waited for my computer to start.

> Colin: I can't stop thinking about you.

> Colin: I'm going to get fired because all I can think about is sex.

Colin: You've turned me into a teenager again.

I grinned.

Me: I'm sorry.

I really wasn't though. It made me hot, knowing he was going to be thinking about me all day.

Colin: I don't think you are. I think you're loving this.

Me: Me?

Colin: Yeah, you.

Colin: And I might be stepping over the line here, but since I usually leave before you, I need to know who you put that outfit on for. I'm guessing it's not any of your cubicle-mates.

Me: There's a new guy at work. He's handsome, young, and single. I thought I'd see if I could catch his attention.

I grinned. It was only partly true. There was a new gentleman who had started, and he was handsome, but he was older than me and married. And I had no interest in him, but I wanted to see what Colin would say.

Colin: Lucky bastard. I'm jealous that he gets to look at you all day.

Me: Well, not all day. I do have to work, you know.

Colin: Right. Work.

Colin: What's work again?

Me: It's that thing you do forty hours a week to earn money and pay the bills.

Colin: Oh yeah.

Colin: I want you to do me a favor.

Me: What's that?

Colin: I want you to flirt with the new guy. Lay it on thick. I want you to make him so hard that he has to cover up the front of his pants. And I want you to remember that you were the one to do that to him.

Colin: Then, before you leave work, I want you to take off your panties and take a picture of your pussy. I want you to stand in front of the new guy, so he can see the picture as you send it to me.

My blush this morning had been nothing compared to the fire I felt in my face right now. I couldn't tell if Colin was serious or if he was calling out my lie. But I didn't have much time to think about it because I wanted to reply right away, as if he hadn't tripped me up.

> Me: How about I just have him take the picture for me? I'm sure he'd get a better angle.

> Colin: As long as he doesn't touch you, I agree.

> Colin: But if you're going to have your own photographer, why don't you make me a little video instead?

> Colin: I want you to stick a finger in your pussy until you're nice and wet, and then I want you to suck it off. Make sure you're looking into the camera the entire time.

My mouth dropped open. He *had* to be messing with me. *Right?*

"*Paisley.*"

I jumped in my seat, and my phone flew out of my hand and onto the floor, landing at my boss's feet, facedown.

She leaned over to pick it up, and I started to sweat.

Oh God, please don't read my texts. Please don't read my texts.

She flipped the phone over, and my home screen showed as she handed it back to me.

My shoulders sagged in relief.

"Are you okay?"

Paisley, you're at work.

I sat up again. "Yes, just my sister, discussing dinner plans. Did you need me for something?"

"I saw you come in, and since you're the first one here, I just wanted you to know that Wendy called in sick."

I attempted a normal smile. "Thanks for letting me know."

My boss eyed me for a few seconds but didn't ask me any more questions. "You're welcome," she said.

As soon as she was gone, I pulled up my messages.

Colin had sent me one more text.

> Colin: And as you're sucking your juices off yourself, I want you to pretend that it's my cock in your mouth and that I just got done fucking you raw, so you're tasting both of us together.

I clutched my phone to my chest and slumped in my seat in defeat.

If he was in front of me, I'd wave a white flag because I couldn't compete.

Maybe I should have put *no dirty talk* on the list.

Chapter Twenty

COLIN

I GOT to Felix and Audrey's house before Paisley, and I was getting a little nervous about seeing her.

I had sent her several *not suitable for work* texts, and I thought she knew I was having fun with her, but she had not replied to the last several I'd sent her. At this point, I wasn't sure if she'd thought I was serious about the new guy she'd made up at work and she was freaking out or if she had realized I knew there was no new love interest, but I'd just gone too far.

"Here."

I looked down to see my brother was handing me a beer.

"Thanks."

"You look like you could use it. Everything going okay at work? They're not sending you off again, are they?"

I took a long sip. "Things are good. And I'm not going

anywhere." *Yet*. I wasn't sure how long it was going to stay that way.

My parents arrived at the same time that Paisley and Audrey's parents showed up.

My mom gave me a hug and kissed me on the cheek. "I've hardly seen you since you've been home."

"Sorry, Mom."

She squeezed my cheeks like I was a kid. "Don't be sorry. Just come over more."

Next, I shook hands with Paisley's dad and mom.

"Darla, Otis, this is my brother, CJ," Felix said.

"You can call me Colin," I corrected. "There are only seven people who call me CJ, and four of them are in this room."

Otis laughed. "Colin it is."

"Audrey, it smells excellent in here," Darla said.

Otis patted his stomach. "I ate a light lunch so that I could fill up on dinner."

Audrey looked at her watch. "You can start eating as soon as Paisley gets here. One of her coworkers called in sick today, so she had to stay a little late at work."

"I was beginning to think she'd ditched us," I joked, but it had seriously crossed my mind.

Several minutes later, Paisley pushed open the front door without knocking. "I'm here. Sorry I'm late."

She was still wearing the outfit. I had wondered if she was late because she had really gone home to change, so I was relieved that I hadn't been such a creep that she found a different outfit.

I was also thinking that her changing would have been a good thing because she still looked as good this evening as she had this morning.

But I needed to stop fantasizing about taking her clothes off and talk to her. I tried to catch her attention, but she wouldn't quite look into my eyes.

Shit. I might not be in the clear as much as I'd thought I was.

I stood back while she said hello to her parents, but when I went to ask her to speak in private, Felix clapped his hands together, and everyone quieted.

"Time to eat."

I sighed. If I took Paisley into another room now, everyone would notice and speculate on what we were talking about. Giving up for now, I pulled out a chair at the large dining room table and sat.

With my legs bent, my phone dug into my leg from my pocket, and I remembered that I could at least text Paisley to see if she was mad at me.

> Me: I didn't hear from you the rest of the day. Did I go too far?

I forced myself to set my phone down, so I wouldn't stare at it while I waited for a response that might not come.

But I was surprised when she sat next to me. There were several seats open, so it seemed she had picked it on purpose.

I leaned over while everyone was distracted with finding their seats. "Are you mad at me?"

Her head flipped around. "No. Why would I be?"

"Because—"

"Paisley, how's the house-shopping going?" my mom asked. "I heard you were looking."

As Felix and Audrey started passing the food around, Paisley said, "It's going well, especially now that I know it's a marathon and not a sprint. I was worried in the beginning, but I've learned there is no rush."

Heads all around the table nodded in understanding, and one by one, people began to tell their home-buying stories. I half-listened, too focused on if Paisley would talk to me or answer my text.

After we all got our food, I felt a hand slide over my leg and into my lap. It was gone as soon as it had gotten there.

I leaned back in my seat to see what Paisley had left there, and just as I saw the bit of lace, my phone buzzed.

"Colin Jasper, you know you're not supposed to have your phone on at the table," my mom chastised me.

I stuffed Paisley's panties she had set in my lap in my pocket as fast as I could manage and picked up my phone. "Sorry, Mom. I'll put it on silent."

Before I could do that, I saw that Paisley had messaged me back in the notification pop-up on my screen.

When I opened my text, I must have made a sound because several eyes turned my way. But not Paisley's. No, she just snickered into her fist as she pretended to cough.

Which wasn't a surprise since she'd sent me a picture of her *vagina*.

Her pretty pink pussy filled my screen, and my dick was as hard as the table that covered my lap.

I had her underwear in my pocket and a photo on my screen, which meant she had done what I'd told her to do in my series of texts, but that also meant she was sitting next to me, bare.

"Sorry, Mom, I have to respond to this real quick."

"It's that important that it can't wait until after dinner?" She sounded exasperated.

"Yes." It was very important.

> Me: I hope you're ready for me to pound that thing until you can't walk tomorrow.

Chapter Twenty-One

PAISLEY

WAITING the appropriate amount of time to check my phone after Colin texted me was torture. But I didn't want anyone to know we were messaging each other.

"How many houses have you looked at now, Paisley?" my sister asked.

I quickly did the math in my head. "Six. Four last weekend and two this week."

I couldn't wait any longer. I looked down in my lap, where my cell sat.

> Colin: I hope you're ready for me to pound that thing until you can't walk tomorrow.

"Are you looking this weekend?"

I was too busy trying not to combust to pay attention to what Audrey was saying. I'd been sexually amped all day because of Colin, and now, I felt like one little graze on my clit, and I might explode.

"*Paisley*."

My head jerked up at the sound of my mother's voice. "Hmm?"

She shook her head and raised her eyebrows. "Your sister asked you a question."

My eyes darted over to Audrey. "Sorry. What did you ask?"

She rolled her eyes. "I asked, are you looking this weekend?"

"Not tomorrow," Colin interjected.

"Why not tomorrow?" Audrey said.

"She has plans," he answered for me again.

Actually, my realtor had plans, but I knew it was his way of reminding me that I was going to be too incapacitated from sex to go do anything.

Audrey opened her mouth, but before my sister could ask more questions, he said, "This is good chicken, Audrey."

She beamed. "Thank you."

He looked at me and sucked the tip of his thumb in his mouth. "It's good, isn't it, Paisley?"

That was it. I couldn't take it anymore.

"Please excuse me. I need to use the bathroom." I pushed back my chair and sprinted for the basement.

"Someone is in a hurry," my dad said.

The lower level of Audrey and Felix's house was

finished with a family room, a bedroom, and a nice bath-room, which I hurried into and shut the door.

I rested my head against the door as my phone vibrated in my hand.

> Colin: You'd better not be touching that pussy without me. If I have to suffer, you have to suffer.

The thought had crossed my mind. I was so horny that I didn't know if I'd be able to finish dinner and make conversation. If I got myself off quick, I would feel more like myself.

I felt around the wall until I found the light switch and flicked it on. Facing the mirror, I lifted my skirt and put a foot up on the counter, so my crotch showed. Then, I placed one finger between my legs and took a picture of my reflection with the other.

I sent it off to Colin.

> Me: Oh yeah? Too bad you're not here to stop me.

> Colin: Call me.

> Me: What?

That was not the response I had expected.

> Colin: Call. Me.

I did as he'd asked and tried to listen through the door. I heard voices, but I couldn't make out what they were saying until Colin picked up his phone.

"This is Colin." He sounded so formal. "It's work. I need to take this," he said to the table.

Footsteps thudded above, and I knew he was coming to me.

"Did you not like my picture?" I teased, still on the phone with him.

"You know I did. Open the door."

I cracked it ajar just as he got to the bottom of the stairs and stalked toward me.

Instinctively, I moved back when he reached me, which allowed him to close us in the bathroom together.

"You are such a brat," he said and kissed me.

Once his lips hit mine, I didn't hold back as I threw my arms around him and tried to climb him.

But Colin pulled away. "We don't have much time."

He spun me back toward the mirror and pushed me until I was leaning over with my hands on it. There were going to be two Paisley-sized handprints tomorrow, and I briefly wondered what my sister and brother-in-law were going to think.

"Won't people be suspicious if we're both down here?" I asked.

Colin lifted my skirt and unzipped his pants. "They think I'm on a work call and that you're in here alone."

He dragged two fingers between my legs, and when he grazed my swollen nub, I yelped.

"Wet already." He pushed the front of his body against mine and grabbed my hair, dragging my head back so I could see his reflection. "But you'd best be quiet, so no one upstairs hears me fuck you."

I nodded as well as I could, and he smiled.

Then, before I realized what was happening, he shoved his cock inside me and pushed a finger down on my clit.

I barely bit my lip before I shattered. My legs shook, and I was hardly able to hold my body up. I zoned out, and when I came back to reality, Colin was staring at me in the mirror.

"I want to do that over and over, but we don't have time. Sorry, baby, but I gotta make this quick."

I made a noise to let him know I was okay with that and let my hands slide down the mirror. I laid my hot face on the cold counter and held on as Colin fucked me from behind. I thought of how long we could stay in the bathroom together, but even with the seconds ticking away, it didn't seem to make much difference to my body.

It knew what it wanted, and it wanted another orgasm from Colin.

I tried to ignore it and just concentrate on getting him off before we got caught, but it didn't matter.

"Come on, Paise. I know you want to come again, and I'm not going to until you do."

Well, if he insisted...

I didn't hold off any longer, and within a minute, I was climaxing again. My legs stopped working, but Colin was there to catch me. He wrapped his arm around my waist and yanked me back toward him as he came too.

He almost fell on top of me as he grunted, but he caught his body with his other arm, and I grinned. I loved hearing him come.

Unfortunately, we didn't have time to waste, basking in our afterglow.

Colin pulled out of me and dropped the condom I hadn't even realized he'd put on in the toilet. He tugged my skirt down and straightened it. He ran his fingers through my hair and placed a soft kiss on my lips.

"Go on up. I'll meet you there."

"What are you going to do?"

"Pretend that I used the bathroom after you."

I nodded. "Good idea. Are you sure I look okay?"

"You look thoroughly fucked."

"Great. The look every mother wants to see on her daughter."

"I'm kidding. You look fine. Your cheeks are a little pink, but I don't think they'll notice."

I turned and checked myself in the mirror. He was right. I didn't look bad. "Can I have my underwear back?"

He chuckled, and I thought he would hand them over, but he told me, "No. They're mine for the night now."

Since we didn't have time to argue, I let it go. I made sure the basement was clear and headed upstairs.

I was relieved when no one paid me much attention or stopped talking to look at me.

I sat back down and started eating, hoping everyone would think I'd been there for longer than I had been.

"Where's Colin?" Felix asked.

"I saw him downstairs. He went into the bathroom after I got out."

"I'm here," Colin said as he reached the top of the stairs. "Sorry about that. Important business," he said as he sat next to me, and I tried not to laugh or blush.

And it seemed like only a minute later, he leaned back in his seat and patted his stomach. "That was delicious."

I looked at him in amazement. "How are you finished already?" I was only halfway done.

"I was starving." He looked at me with hooded eyes and lowered his voice. "You'd better eat up too. You're going to need your strength."

"We already did it today," I whispered back.

"After five, it's the weekend. I get you twice today." He raised his brow. "Unless you don't want to."

I didn't say another word.

Chapter Twenty-Two

PAISLEY

SATURDAY MORNING, I climbed out of bed at a good hour. And despite the vigorous sex Colin and I'd had last night, I was still able to walk. Although I was feeling the effects of our late-night activities, so Colin hadn't been totally wrong.

When I walked into the living room on the way to the kitchen, I saw a T-shirt lying on the arm of the couch. There was another one thrown on the coffee table, and I gritted my teeth. Colin was always taking his shirts off and leaving them around the house. For some reason, he was always hot.

I tried to ignore the clothes and move on, but there was another hanging on the back of a chair in the kitchen. Did he even have any shirts in his closet or dresser, or were they all out here?

Let it go, Paisley.

Taking my own advice, I started the coffee and made

myself some oatmeal for breakfast. But when I went to the fridge to add milk to it, I discovered the carton was empty. I groaned in frustration.

Seriously irritated now, I ran around the house, picking up all of Colin's shirts. I even found one in the hall bathroom, which was technically mine.

I marched up to his bedroom door, flung it open, and threw his clothes at his head.

Most of them missed, but one covered his whole face, and I felt a sense of satisfaction.

Colin ripped the cloth off his face. "What the hell was that for?"

"For leaving your damn clothes all over the house." I slammed the door and whipped it back open. "And for drinking all the damn milk and putting the damn carton back," I yelled.

He was up on his elbow by now. "Oh, that?" He grinned. "Yeah, I did that on purpose."

"What the hell for?"

"Just making sure you don't fall in love with me."

"You're impossible," I retorted and closed the door again.

"I think you mean, irresistible," he shouted through the wood.

"In your dreams."

"Paise. *Paisley*."

I sighed and opened his door again. "What?" I bit out.

"Can you fold my shirts for me?"

"Asshole," I said and turned to leave.

"I'm just kidding. There's more milk in the back of the fridge."

I narrowed my eyes at him.

He held his hands up. "I promise."

"You're lucky."

"How's that?" he asked.

"I was going to go get my oatmeal and throw that at you next."

———

My realtor only had time to show Colin and me one house later that day because she had other plans in the evening.

"Oh my gosh, this place is so cute," I said.

"That's why I made time to show it to you. It's new to the market, but it has so many things you're looking for," Sloan said.

And there were things that Colin couldn't dispute either. The kitchen was a nice size, it had a two-stall garage, it was a ranch-style home so there was a bathroom on the main floor, and it had three bedrooms. It wasn't the biggest house, but three bedrooms sold better than two.

The interior hadn't been updated in about ten years, so it wasn't the fanciest house, but the furnishings were fairly modern, and I could picture my stuff there.

Sloan handed me the homebuyer sheet. "It just got a new roof three years ago, and it's in a good school district. Always important when reselling even if you don't have your own kids."

Colin had been fairly quiet, so I dared to look at him. "What do you think?"

"It's a good place."

"Really?" I turned back to Sloan. "He always has something to complain about."

"Hey. I don't complain. I criticize," he said.

"I stand corrected."

Sloan chuckled and looked at her phone. "I hate to kick you two out so soon, but my husband isn't very happy that I'm here at all. I promised him a Saturday with no work, and we have dinner reservations. I apologize."

"No, I understand. I'm glad you took the time to show me. I'm excited."

"You have a lot to think about."

Sloan walked us out and locked up the house.

As we strode to Colin's car, he said, "It's almost six. Did you want to stop somewhere and eat while you think?"

Not having to worry about making anything when we got home sounded great. "Yes, please." I had enough to think about as it was.

————

Colin and I agreed on a place that had good burgers and plenty of beer. I was hoping a little alcohol would help me relax. Since it was Saturday and all the tables were taken, we opted to sit at the bar, so we didn't have to wait.

"It's a good house, Paise," Colin said, nodding toward the spec sheet in front of me.

I studied his face. He seemed almost sad, but maybe it was because he was showing me he was being serious about the home.

"It is, but I'm nervous. Realistically, I know I'm buying a house, but it seemed almost surreal, and now, it seems more tangible. I have never purchased something that costs this much money. I don't know if I'm ready."

Colin covered my hand with his. "You'll be fine. People do it every day."

"I know. It's just—"

"Paisley."

I froze at the sound of my name. The voice was very familiar, but there was no way.

Slowly, I turned around until I saw who the speaker was, and when I did, I wanted to run out of the restaurant and never look back.

But I simply smiled politely and said, "Hello, Ron."

"Who's this?" He pointed to Colin, and I could tell he'd had a little too much to drink.

"This is Colin. Colin, this is Ron. We used to be...friends."

Ron snorted. "Yeah, until she went crazy."

"Thanks for stopping by. See you later," I said to him, hoping he'd get the hint and leave.

He completely ignored me, his focus on Colin, but I could barely look at him, afraid of what Ron was going to say next.

"We were friends until we had sex. Then, it was like cling city, man. She wouldn't leave me alone."

My face burned with embarrassment, but I tried to play it cool.

"I think you're exaggerating," Colin said.

Ron got right in Colin's face. "Do. Not. Sleep. With. Her. She'll think you're her boyfriend, and before you know it, she'll think she's in love with you." Ron wobbled on his feet as he stepped back. "And don't just take my word for it. I heard the last guy she dated called her a stalker."

And I was done.

Even if Colin and I weren't dating, I didn't want him to hear about how much of a loser I'd been in the past. Sure, I'd told him I fell in love too fast, but it was humiliating for him to hear what my exes thought of me.

I grabbed my purse. Since Ron wasn't going away, I guessed that meant I was.

But Colin's solid hand landed on mine, and he shook his head. Putting his arm around me, he pulled me close and pushed Ron back a step.

"I'm already sleeping with her. I'm already her boyfriend. And I'm the one who fell in love with her first. Just because you were too blind to see what a good thing you had doesn't mean you have to talk shit about her to someone else. So you didn't like her. I do. I love her even. So, why don't you go back to where you came from, finish your beer, and go home to your one and only girlfriend, Rosy?"

"Rosy?" Ron scoffed.

Colin rolled his eyes. "It's not funny when you have to

explain the joke," he said under his breath. He raised his voice. "Yeah, Rosy, as in rosy palm."

Ron stared at him blankly.

"You're going to go home and masturbate because it's the only thing that wants to sleep with you. Jesus, how drunk are you?"

Ron stuck out his middle finger. "Fuck you. And I have a fiancée."

"Good one. Send her my condolences," Colin said. "Now, will you leave us alone? We're trying to have a date here."

Ron had the look of someone who wanted to say more, but you could tell that nothing came to mind.

It was enough for Colin because he twirled us both around in our stools to face away from him.

He put his arm back around me. "I'm sorry you had to deal with that."

"I'm sorry you had to hear it." I looked up into his eyes. "Thanks for pretending to be with me."

"Paisley, anyone would be lucky to be with you. That guy's an asshole, and he doesn't know what he's missing."

Chapter Twenty-Three

COLIN

PAISLEY LOOKED AWAY, but I put my finger under her chin and turned her face back to mine.

"I'm serious. You are a wonderful person. Just because he didn't get you doesn't mean you're not worth being with." I gestured in her ex's direction, where he was with a group of guys. "You can do so much better than that."

"Thank you," she whispered. I didn't hear her over the loud music, but I could read her lips.

I leaned down and kissed her long and thoroughly. It was probably something a boyfriend would do, but I didn't care. I wanted her to *feel* I meant what I'd said.

"Do you want to go put our name in for a table? Or we could go to another restaurant? I don't want you to be uncomfortable during dinner."

"If we stay here, will you keep pretending to be into me? Or is that petty?"

Baby, I'm already into you. "Deal. And after what he

said about you to a stranger, I think you deserve to have a boyfriend tonight. But you have to do something for me."

"What's that?"

"Try to forget about him?"

She smiled. "Deal."

———

Even though Paisley had seemed to perk up after my pep talk, by the time we got home from the restaurant, it seemed like it had worn off. It probably didn't help that it was pouring rain outside, and walking the short distance from the restaurant doors to the car had us soaked.

"I think I'm going to go to bed early."

She looked defeated, and I hated that for her.

"I have a better idea," I said.

She smiled, but it didn't reach her eyes. "If you're thinking sex, I'm going to have to politely decline. I know we haven't done the deed today, and I'm sorry, but—"

"No, I wasn't talking about sex." I was a little insulted she would think that I wanted that from her when she clearly wasn't in the mood. However, she was upset, so I tried not to take it personally. "It's been a few days since we watched *Charmed*, and I thought we could do that together. I still don't know if Leo is good or bad, and I'd really like to know."

"Wow, you're really invested."

"I suppose I am. But why watch a show if you don't care what happens?"

"That is true."

I lifted my chin toward the hall. "Go put your pajamas on. We can make it a PJ party. I think we have popcorn and ice cream."

"How are we going to have a PJ party when you don't wear anything to bed?"

"How do you know I don't wear anything to bed? Maybe I get dressed after you leave my room or I leave yours."

"You told me the night you came home drunk."

"That seems about right. But I do own sweatpants. I will find something comfortable to put on."

She stood there for a few seconds after considering my idea. "After running into my ex, I suppose it would be nice to binge on junk food. I've never done it with a guy before."

I grinned. "There's a first time for everything."

———

"*Colin.*"

My eyes snapped open, and I tried to shake off the deep sleep I'd just been taken from. "What?"

"We fell asleep on the couch," Paisley said.

She was right. I was on my back with Paisley halfway on top of me. I didn't even remember getting sleepy, much less dozing off.

I closed my eyes. "Mmm," I said in response. "I'm too

tired to get up." I squeezed her around her waist. "Plus, you're nice and warm."

At some point while watching TV, we'd grabbed a blanket to cuddle underneath. It wasn't any wonder we had fallen asleep.

"But we're not supposed to sleep together."

"Technically, your rule says we're not supposed to sleep in each other's beds." I yawned and knew sleep was going to pull me back under again. "I'm too tired to move. But if you feel more comfortable getting up, I understand."

I didn't wait for her to respond and let slumber overtake me.

When I woke up in the morning, light was peeking through the living room blinds, and Paisley was fast asleep on my chest.

Looking up to the ceiling, I smiled.

She'd stayed.

Chapter Twenty-Four

PAISLEY

"SO, how is your practice subject doing?" Alexis asked.

"What? Who?" I asked.

It was Wednesday night, our monthly dinner, and it was time to play catch-up in each other's lives.

"Colin. I thought you'd texted us all and said you were going to sleep with him."

I chuckled. "Oh yeah." I grinned like the Cheshire cat. "I have. Many times."

"Ooh," several of my friends said.

"Was it as good as the first time?" Bree asked.

"Yes. And then some." I sighed. "He's amazing in bed."

Bree grinned at me. "I hear that."

Tessa cringed, and I laughed. I was really glad I had a sister sometimes.

"How are the rules going?" Elizabeth asked.

"Rules?" Tessa asked.

"Didn't I message everyone the rules?" I asked. I thought I had, but then again, I had been distracted by sex.

"No," Tessa said, clearly not happy about the fact.

I grabbed my phone, pulled up the list of rules, and handed them over to her.

She cleared her throat. "*Number one: No sleeping in the same bed together. We have sex, and then the other goes back to his or her bed.*"

"Good rule," Bree said. "Sharing a bed with Zack was probably part of the reason I fell for him."

Pru snorted. "That and his pierced dong," she said.

Bree grinned. "It didn't hurt."

"*Ladies,*" Tessa said. "He's my *brother.*"

"Sorry," Pru said even though she clearly wasn't. When Tessa looked down, she made the blow-job gesture at Bree, who nodded.

I had to cover my mouth, so I didn't crack up laughing.

Tessa, either oblivious to or ignoring our friends, continued, "*Rule number two: No dates.*" She nodded. "Very good rule. *Number three: No pet names. Number four: No being boyfriend-y. No buying me gifts or texting to ask how my day is.* I'm guessing these are examples?"

I nodded. "Yeah. There's obviously more to it, but I couldn't list them all."

"*Number five: You have to keep your promise about helping me not fall in love with you.*" Tessa set the phone down.

"I explained my problem and why I couldn't sleep with him again. He offered to help me not fall in love with him."

"And how is that going?" Tessa asked.

I gritted my teeth. "He has clothes lying all over the house, he finishes the coffee that I started without making more, and he leaves dishes in the sink."

Bree and Tessa laughed.

"That's just normal man stuff," Bree said.

"I think he's doing it on purpose."

Of course, then he also did things like cook dinner for me, buy my favorite yogurt when he went grocery shopping, and give me the most fantastic orgasms.

"For someone who falls in love easily, it's amazing you've never lived with a man before," Isabelle said.

"Which just shows that this whole experiment with Colin is the right thing to do," Elizabeth said.

I supposed she was right. The only man I'd ever lived with before Colin was my dad, and he'd lived with three females, so he had been outnumbered.

"I have to agree that there are some things that men just do and aren't necessarily meant to annoy you on purpose." Alexis curled her lip. "But some men do it more than others."

I nodded sympathetically. Her ex-husband was an asshole and had probably been horrible to live with.

Alexis shifted in her seat, clearly uncomfortable with getting pity. "Keep reading," she said to Tessa.

Tessa lifted my phone after I had to unlock it again. "*Rule six: No kissing.*"

Several of my friends gasped.

"But kissing is the best," Alexis said.

I quickly waved my hands in the air. "It was just a thought, but it's not one Colin and I are actually following."

"So, why is it on there?" Alexis asked.

I looked at Isabelle.

She shrugged. "I was thinking *Pretty Woman*."

"Ahhh," everyone said in understanding.

"It was a good idea," I agreed, "but Colin and I had already kissed the first night we were together. Seemed weird to go back after that." Or it just seemed wrong not to kiss him in the moment.

Tessa cleared her throat. "And last but not least, rule number seven. They can only have sex four times a week."

Bree wrinkled her nose, and Tessa shook her head.

"We actually negotiated that one," I said. "We agreed to have sex once a day during the week and twice on the weekends."

"That seems like a strange rule," Pru said. "I feel like it shouldn't have a limit."

"This is Paisley we're talking about," Elizabeth said. "It was my idea because I didn't want her to be in an orgasm haze around him. I think that's what causes her to fall in love half the time."

Pru nodded. "That is an excellent point."

Despite agreeing, it did make me feel foolish. I didn't think I was ruled by my body that much. But then again, history had proven I was.

"So, how's it going with those rules?" Pru asked.

Um...

"Pretty good."

If you didn't count going out to dinner on Saturday, where we'd literally pretended to be dating, or how we had fallen asleep on the couch together. Also, Colin had called me baby twice—but only twice—during sex, and he had started shortening my name to Paise, but that was a nickname, not a pet name.

I bit my lip.

I hoped I wasn't getting in over my head. "I haven't fallen in love with him yet." But I could see how a woman would.

"Pretty good? That's it?" Tessa said.

I didn't really want to talk about Colin and me for some reason, but if I said that, everyone was going to think I was hiding something.

"Okay, it's good. Better than good. He's great in bed, and so far, I haven't fallen into my old habits."

Tessa grinned. "That's what I like to hear."

I looked at Bree. "How's the engagement party coming along?"

"Great. My mother is happy with the dinner idea, and she doesn't know about the party afterward."

Tessa gasped and looked at me. "You should bring Colin to the engagement party."

Pru looked at Tessa like she wasn't thinking. "That sure seems like dating to me. Isn't that one step away from a wedding?"

"But I want to meet him," Tessa complained.

I had to agree with Pru. I couldn't ask Colin to go to an engagement party.

"Let me see what I can do about you meeting him," I said. I didn't have any ideas in mind, but I was sure I could come up with a plan.

"Speaking of engagements and weddings, I have to tell you all something," Bree said and gave us an uncomfortable smile.

"Oh no," Isabelle said.

"It's not bad. I just don't want to hurt anyone," Bree explained.

Pru motioned with her hand. "Just spit it out."

"Zack and I don't want a big wedding—"

Alexis gasped. "Oh my God, we're not invited."

"You're invited," Bree said. "Please let me finish."

Alexis put her hands up. "Sorry. Please continue."

"You're all invited, but we're only going to have a maid of honor and a best man. And since Tessa is Zack's sister, she's going to be the maid of honor. Or rather the matron of honor. Don't hate me."

Alexis scoffed. "That's it? As long as we're invited, we understand."

"But do we?" I joked.

Bree's eyes widened.

"I'm kidding," I quickly said. "With your mom and everything, I can see why you'd want to keep your wedding small and easy. No hard feelings."

Bree put a hand to her chest. "Thank you for understanding."

"But who's going to be the best man?" Pru asked. "Since neither of you has a brother."

"Sebastian. He is my cousin and was the closest thing I had to a brother, growing up. And since he moved back to Minnesota, he and Zack have become friends."

Pru wrinkled her nose, but I thought Sebastian was the perfect fit since he was family, like Tessa.

"Hey, Paisley, does the *no texting* thing include sexting?" Tessa asked as she looked at my phone with raised eyebrows.

Oh no. Had she seen the texts Colin and I'd exchanged last weekend? My phone had surely locked again, and it wasn't like she'd been going through it.

All eyes turned to me.

"No, it doesn't count."

"What does it say?" Alexis asked.

"*I hate to tell you this, but your bed is ruined.*"

"What?" I snatched my phone from her hands.

"Damn, Paisley, what did you and Colin do in it?" Pru asked.

"He can't be talking about sex," I said. "We had sex on the kitchen counter last night."

Alexis snapped her fingers. "Someone should have come up with the rule that Paisley could only have sex missionary-style in a bed. Kitchen sex will ruin any woman."

My friends laughed, but I was too busy waiting for

Colin to text me back after I messaged him to ask what had happened.

"Oh no," I said when the next message came through.

"What's wrong?" Isabelle asked first.

I looked up. "You know how it rained hard for a few days? The roof leaked, and now, my bed is covered by a big chunk of the ceiling that fell."

Chapter Twenty-Five

PAISLEY

WHEN I GOT HOME, I barely had my car parked and my keys out of the ignition before I sprinted into the house.

Colin was standing at the end of the hallway, looking into my bedroom, running his hand on the back of his head.

When he saw me come in, he straightened his spine and looked guilt-ridden.

"Paise, I am so sorry this happened," he said when I reached him, but I was too busy looking into my bedroom to respond.

Colin had sent me a picture with his news, but I had only briefly looked at it before I rushed out of the building.

There was a large chunk of plaster on my bed. I looked up to see a hole with a dark stain surrounding it, which had to be from water. Two men were in the room with clip-boards, and every time they moved, there was a squishing sound on the carpet.

"Being gone a year, I should have known to get the roof looked at when I got home. It had crossed my mind a couple of times with winter around the corner, but I kept forgetting to call someone."

I put my hand on Colin's arm. "Colin, please. It was an accident, and it looks like most of the damage is to my bed. I'm not mad at you."

"Well, I'm mad at me."

I looked up to the damage again. I supposed he was. He was going to pay a lot more money than I was.

A stampede of footsteps sounded behind us, and we both turned to see my friends.

"What are you doing here?" I asked.

"You took off so we followed you, and we wanted to make sure you were okay," Tessa said. She peeked around the corner. "Eek. I guess not."

"Let's go into the living room," I suggested since the hall was too small for all of us to stand there.

One by one, my friends looked into my bedroom before following Colin and me into the living room.

"Colin, these are my friends." I introduced them and collapsed onto the couch.

"Sorry I ruined your dinner," he said. "I know you ladies only get together once a month."

"I think this was Mother Nature's doing," Isabelle said.

"I hope you have good insurance," Elizabeth said.

Colin chuckled. "I do, and thankfully, I knew who to call to get someone out here right away. Unfortunately, it will probably take a week or so to fix, and Paisley's bed is toast."

"It's a good thing you're looking to move," Alexis joked.

Colin stiffened, but I snorted.

"That's a ways off," I said.

"What about the house we saw on Saturday?" he asked.

My friends all looked at me.

"You didn't tell us about the house," Pru said.

Probably because we had been too busy talking about Colin.

"We didn't get that far. We didn't even order any food."

"I noticed," Tessa muttered, rubbing her pregnant belly.

"You all go eat," I said to my friends. "I don't want to keep Baby Crawford waiting."

Tessa sat down next to me. "We're not leaving you."

"You go," Colin said to me.

I shook my head. "No. I don't want you to deal with this alone."

My friends exchanged looks.

"Then, we'll all eat here," Pru said.

"I volunteer to go and pick up food," Bree said.

"I'll go with to help," Alexis offered.

Pru smiled at me. "It looks like we're staying."

———

COLIN

Despite the situation in Paisley's bedroom, I had a good time with Paisley's friends. One of them even offered the contractor and his assistant something to eat, but they declined.

We were cleaning up our food containers, and I said, "Thanks for dinner. I appreciate it."

Part of me was still freaking out about the leaking-roof situation, so the temporary distraction was nice.

"It's the least we could do," the friend Tessa said. "Also, it's been a long time since we did a weekly dinner at home. We always go out to eat."

"Yeah, this was fun," her other friend Bree said. "Paisley didn't tell us how cool her roommate was."

I laughed. "I don't know about that."

"You were cool enough to let her stay here," Isabelle pointed out.

I looked at Paisley. "It wasn't a hard decision."

"See. Cool," Bree said. "You know, Colin, I'd love to have you join us at to my engagement party. We'll all be there. There will be food and dancing. It'll be fun."

Tessa clapped her hands. "You should totally come."

I turned to Paisley, whose eyes were huge. "Is that okay with you?"

"Yes."

"Then, why do you look like you want me to say no?"

"Oh. This?" She circled her face. "This is because my

friends supposedly hate men, yet they're inviting you to a celebration."

I laughed. "What?" I asked, confused.

"We hate *asshole* men," Pru clarified.

"It's a long story," Paisley said. "Just know, you must be pretty special."

I grinned. Paisley had called me special.

"When is it?" I asked Bree.

She gave me a date that was coming up soon.

"I'll be there."

Tessa yawned. "I'm sorry to eat and run, but I'd better get home before I fall asleep, driving. This baby makes me super tired."

"Tell Seth hi," someone said to her as she left.

"Will do." Tessa closed the door.

"I'm going to go too," Bree said.

"Same here," Elizabeth said, and soon, everyone was saying the same thing.

"Go, go," Paisley said. "Go home and enjoy your beds."

Her friends laughed, and a few minutes later, they left. Now that everyone was gone, I was reminded of the mess I had to deal with and how Paisley didn't have a room to stay in because of it.

"So, about your sleeping situation, since your bed is ruined, why don't you take mine tonight, and I'll sleep out here? If you can't find anything to sleep in, I have a T-shirt you can wear. I plan to take tomorrow off work and get as much of your stuff out of your room as I can. Shit, I hope you can find something to wear for work tomorrow." I ran my hand over my face. "This fucking sucks."

Paisley stepped forward and pulled my arm down. "Honest question for you."

"Okay."

"Besides your roof being in perfect condition, what do you want to happen tonight? Do you want to sleep on the couch?"

Maybe I should have lied, but I didn't.

Grabbing her hips, I pulled her to me. "You sleeping in my bed with me. Naked. With me inside you half the night because it's the only peace I'm going to get for a while."

She slipped her arms around my neck. "Let's do that then."

I leaned back to study her face. "Which part?"

"All of it."

Chapter Twenty-Six

PAISLEY

"THANKS FOR MEETING ME HERE," Sloan said to me.

She had asked me to meet her in her office, so I'd come directly from work.

"What did you want to see me about?"

She slid a piece of paper in front of me. And then another.

One was the great house Colin and I had looked at on Saturday. The other was a house I hadn't seen before.

I looked up at my realtor.

"The house on the left had an offer come in last night and another this morning."

My eyebrows shot up. *That was fast.*

"The house on the right just came on the market. It has all the same things as the other house. It's just in a different neighborhood." She tilted her head.

I wasn't sure if she was waiting for me to respond or if she was studying me.

Probably both.

I cleared my throat. "Well, as I said, there was an incident at Colin's house. Things are kind of wild right now."

Elbows on her armrests, Sloan folded her hands in front of her. "This happened on Wednesday, correct?"

"Yes."

"So, you had Sunday, Monday, and Tuesday to put in an offer," she said, clearly waiting for an explanation.

I opened my mouth, but I couldn't find a good reason for my hesitation.

Sloan looked down her nose, her expression serious. "Do you even want to buy a house, Paisley?"

"Yes," I immediately said. But then I slumped in my chair. "I don't know."

"Thank you for being honest. What's the problem?"

I let my head fall against the back of the chair. "A man."

"Oh." Sloan sounded genuinely surprised. "I didn't realize. Does this have to do with Colin, your roommate?"

Big sigh. "Yes."

"Because he's not just a roommate?"

"Yes." I sat up. "But I don't know what he is."

"I've been there," she said under her breath, but I was too far gone in my head to ask her what she was referring to.

Instead, I had diarrhea of the mouth, and I couldn't stop myself.

"My landlord kicked me out of my house at the last minute because he'd decided to sell. I didn't have anyplace to go—and I didn't want to live with my parents—so my sister offered me her brother-in-law's place since he was out of the country on business for several months. After I moved in, I went to a party for work, met a guy in the hotel bar, and had a one-night stand with him. Some weeks later, the brother-in-law came back into town, and surprise." I flashed my hands in front of me for effect. "He was the guy I'd slept with from the hotel."

"Oh, wow."

"But my friends and I are part of this silly club where we've sworn off men for different reasons. Mine is that I fall in love too fast, especially with guys I sleep with. So, I was really proud of myself for leaving Colin after the night at the hotel even though he was the best sex I'd ever had, ya know?"

Sloan, with her eyes wide, nodded slowly, as if she was worried I was going to freak out.

"So, it turned out, he was my new roommate, my new landlord, my new whatever. The point is, we were living together. And I was used to guys trying to get rid of me, but Colin? Noooooo, he wanted to have sex with me again. What was I supposed to do with that?" I said, throwing my hands up.

"I—"

"So, a few of my friends and I came up with rules for us to sleep with each other because we all decided Colin would be good practice for me not to fall in love. But you know what happened with those rules?"

"I have no id—"

"We broke them," I blurted out. "We broke every single one of those rules. We kiss, he calls me Paise, we're going to an engagement party together, he takes care of me, we have sex all the time, and we're sharing a bed every night because the roof collapsed on mine. And now..." I stuck out my bottom lip. "And now, I'm really starting to like him."

"Starting?"

I frowned.

Sloan sat forward. "I think we need to put your house situation on hold."

"Yeah, I think that's best." I picked up my purse from the floor. "Sorry I let everything out like that. If you never want to work with me again, I understand."

She smiled, her eyes filled with kindness. "I'm not going to fire you as a client." She held up a finger. "As long as you're serious about buying a home." Dropping her hand, she said, "I just don't know if you are."

"I don't know either. But I can't keep living with Colin. He didn't ask for all this." I waved my hands up and down in front of my body.

"He kind of did."

"That's just sex. Men always want to sleep with me, but they never want to stick around."

"Colin kind of seems like he does." She tapped her temple. "Think about it. And maybe talk to him."

Knowing she was right, I nodded and left her office with a lot on my mind.

I was all set to talk to Colin, but when I got home, he

was in the middle of helping the construction crew. He was rubbing his forehead, and he looked stressed. He must have sensed me though because he lifted his head and turned my way.

"Hey," he said, the corner of his mouth turning up but the smile didn't reach his eyes. "How did it go? Did you look at any good houses?"

"Yeah. One was great," I said, thinking of the home-buyer sheets Sloan had placed in front of me. I should have told him I was putting a pause on the whole thing, but I didn't want to add to his problems. I lifted the grocery bag in my hand. "I bought stuff for dinner."

"Thank you."

"You're welcome."

Someone said Colin's name, and I turned and headed to the kitchen without another word.

Chapter Twenty-Seven

COLIN

FOR THE PAST WEEK, the renovations in Paisley's room had taken up most of my spare time when I wasn't at work. Paisley had gone to look at houses one night on her own, and most nights, she was nice enough to find us food, so we didn't starve.

The construction team was set to finish up tomorrow, and I was hoping things would get back to normal. No more banging from the crew from morning till night, and Paisley's stuff wouldn't have to sit in the living room any longer.

But I had to admit, sharing a bed with her was almost worth the damage. This morning, she'd woken me up with her mouth on my dick. I loved when she let me fuck her mouth. And as a thank-you, I'd had her ride my face until I could barely breathe. It would have been a good way to die.

Feeling good about my house being fixed, I wasn't prepared for my boss to walk by my door.

"Black, my office."

I sighed, got up from my drafting table, and followed him.

"What's going on?" I asked after shutting the door behind us.

"I need you to head up the project in St. Louis," my boss, Arnold, said.

No, no, no. Panic immediately flooded my body. The St. Louis project would start in less than a month. I had just gotten home.

"I thought Adams was heading that up. And I'm still working on my current project."

"Adams's wife is having surgery, and he wants to stay in town while she recovers. He'll take over your project here when you head down to St. Louis."

Unclenching my jaw, I asked, "How long do you think I'll be there?"

"It's a yearlong project. Eighteen months tops."

I'd just gotten home from being gone a year.

"You're not happy," Arnold said.

"Not really, no. I haven't been back that long, and you're already sending me out again."

My boss leaned back in his chair. "When I hired you, I hired you to travel, did I not?"

"You did," I admitted.

"Okay then. Do the work I hired you for." Arnold got up from his chair, came around to me, and slapped my back. "Look on the bright side. With this trip, at least you'll be stateside, so you can come home to visit your parents a lot more."

I didn't say another word. I wasn't sure I would be able to say something I wouldn't regret because I was pissed.

When I got back to my own office, I shoved the door closed and paced.

I considered that it was time to find a different job. I hated the idea of starting over, but I hated the idea of moving away for another year even more.

An image of Paisley flashed through my mind. Of her finding someone else to fall in love with while I was away.

I shook thoughts of her away. Even without Paisley, I was tired of doing what I was doing. I wanted something more permanent. I wanted to get married and start a family. I couldn't raise children if I was gone for twelve months at a time. And I couldn't ask a wife to uproot herself from her own job and move.

I took a deep breath, got behind my desk, and opened my laptop. I was just typing in my job search when I got a text from Paisley.

> Paisley: How does Chinese food sound tonight? It's a little early to celebrate, but I don't feel like cooking.

> Me: Sounds good.

> Paisley: Are you okay?

> Me: I'll be fine. Just not in the mood to celebrate anything.

> Paisley: What happened?

I tapped my phone against my hand. Should I tell her what was going on? Was that too serious? Too "boyfriend-y"?

I honestly didn't know if I cared that much at the moment. What was the worst that might happen? That she'd move out and move on with her life? She was planning to do that anyway.

Fuck it.

> Me: My boss just informed me that I have to go to St. Louis for another year. I'd leave at the beginning of next month.

> Paisley: And you don't want to go?

> Me: Goddammit, no. I'm so tired. I'm tired of leaving for months at a time. It was fun in the beginning, but I want to be home.

> Paisley: Have you thought about telling your boss that?

Considering how I had pointed out I had just come back to Minnesota, I didn't think he would care.

Me: It's pointless. My coworker's wife is having surgery, so I'm getting sent in his place. My boss thinks that because I'm the single guy, I'm easy to move around.

Paisley: That's so wrong.

Me: The irony is, I'll never get a wife if I can't stay in one place.

Paisley: Do you want to get married?

Me: Yes. I've always pictured myself as a family man. This bachelor lifestyle is getting old.

Paisley: I didn't know you felt that way.

Me: Yeah, well, it seems a little much, like something a boyfriend would tell you, right?

Was that comment a little mean? Perhaps, but I was feeling bitter.

Paisley: No. It sounds like something a friend would talk about with another friend. You know so much about me, and I never asked what you wanted out of life in return.

Paisley: I'm so used to guys wanting to be single and pushing me away that it seems I forgot that not all men feel that way.

Paisley: I'm sorry I never asked.

Me: Don't be sorry. I never exactly offered either.

Paisley: What are you going to do? You can't stay at your job. The money is not worth the misery.

Me: You're right, which is why I'm already looking for another one.

Paisley: Good for you.

Me: Thanks.

Paisley: Is there anything I can do to help you feel better? Want me to kick your boss's ass?

A genuine laugh burst out of me, and I smiled.

Me: Tempting, but he's a sixty-something-year-old man. I don't think it would be fair.

Paisley: He's not treating you fair, so he deserves it.

"God, I love you."

The words came out of me without even thinking.

Quickly, I looked down to make sure I hadn't accidentally called her or sent a voice message even though I knew I hadn't.

"I love you," I said again, testing the words on my tongue. It had been a long time since I had said something like that to a woman I was dating. I snorted. And I wasn't even dating Paisley.

To be honest, I wasn't sure I really even did love her. But I definitely knew there was the potential to fall in love with her.

> Paisley: Seriously though, is there anything I can do for you?

Since neither of us was ready for me to say anything about love to her, I naturally shoved it down and turned the conversation toward sex.

> Me: Yes.

> Paisley: What is it?

> Me: I haven't slept with anyone besides you since our first night together, and you've been in my bed every night this past week. I want to take you bare. Nothing between us.

I wished I could see her face, but I'd have to settle for her response. I had seen her pills in the main bathroom, so

I knew birth control wasn't a problem. But it would be a good reason to tell me no, and I wouldn't call her out if she lied to me.

Yet she completely surprised me.

Paisley: I want that too.

Chapter Twenty-Eight

PAISLEY

I CRAWLED up Colin's body and placed a leg on each side of his hips. Gripping his hard dick, I pumped him in my fist a few times just to watch him react. I didn't think I would ever get sick of the way he sucked in his breath and closed his eyes at my touch.

"I already had a shitty day at work. Why are you torturing me?" he asked.

"Not torture. Delaying gratification."

"You're evil."

Truth be told, there was only going to be one first time without a condom, and I wanted it to be special. I wanted to savor the moment. But I was too scared to tell him that.

I placed the length of him between my legs, where I was wet, and rocked my hips over him.

"Mmm, that feels so good," Colin said, slipping a thumb over my clit. "Keep doing that until you come."

"But I thought you didn't want to wait?" His touch felt amazing, and I didn't know if *I* wanted to wait.

"What happened to delayed gratification?" He pulled his hand away. "Maybe I'm giving you too much, too soon."

"I think you're teasing me now, and it's working."

I lifted my pelvis, grabbed his cock to place it at my entrance, and sank down onto him.

"Mary, mother of God," Colin cursed.

"I didn't know you were religious."

"Only when I'm inside you." He grasped my hips. "Now, why don't you ride me until we both see Jesus?"

———

As we lay there on our backs, breathing hard, I picked up Colin's hand and intertwined our fingers.

"How did the job search go?" I asked.

He ran his thumb back and forth over mine. "It went well. Would I have loved the perfect job to show up and to think, *This is the one*? Of course, but that doesn't usually happen on the first day of searching."

"I'm sorry."

"Why are you sorry? It's not your fault."

I shrugged. "Because I feel for you."

"That's appreciated, but it's still not your fault."

He kissed the back of my hand and placed it on his bare chest. It was warm, and I had to admit that I liked lying there with him. I was actually grateful that even though the house would be finished tomorrow, I still wouldn't have a bed.

"Did you apply to any? Or are you going to wait until a better job comes along?" I held my breath as I paused for an answer.

When he'd told me he was supposed to go out of town again, my heart had sunk. I didn't want him to go.

He chuckled. "I applied to all of them."

"You did?" I couldn't stop the smile from spreading across my face.

"I did. Let's hope one of them reaches out to me."

"I'm sure more than one will."

"We'll see."

Turning on my side to face him, I said, "I still think you should tell your boss you're looking for other work. Give them a chance to keep you."

"I don't know."

"It's worth giving them a shot. Unless you don't want to stay."

"I honestly don't know."

"It's something to think about."

Colin met my eyes and almost whispered, "Do you not want me to leave?"

I shook my head. "No, I don't."

Untangling our hands, he rolled me onto my back and moved between my legs. With one slick move, he thrust inside me.

No more words were spoken the rest of the night. Our bodies did all the communicating.

Chapter Twenty-Nine

COLIN

A FEW DAYS LATER, I woke up to the sun shining through my bedroom window, a calm silence of no construction, and Paisley in my arms.

I kissed her forehead. "Paise, Paise, I need you to wake up."

She shoved her nose deeper into my neck and yanked the covers over her head.

Chuckling, I tugged them back down. "Sleepyhead, it's already after nine."

"But I'm so comfy."

"But I need to talk to you."

She ran her hand down my chest and over my hip until she found my dick. It had been soft, but it grew hard the second she touched me.

"You minx. That's not what I meant. I need to speak to you for real."

Letting go of my hard-on, she rolled onto her back. "This sounds serious."

"It is, depending on how you look at it."

"Are you kicking me out?"

The thought was so absurd that I burst out laughing. Paisley frowned.

"I'm sorry. No, I'm not kicking you out."

"It's not really that funny, but go on. What is so important that you woke me from my beauty sleep?"

"You're already beautiful, but I was wondering where you stood on the house-hunting business."

She looked away. "Um…it's the same as it has been."

"What happened to that great house your realtor took special time out to show us? The one that was almost perfect?"

"Uh…"

"Paisley?"

She lifted her head and winced. "It sold."

"I see."

"What does that mean?"

"Is there a reason you didn't try and buy it? Did you even have your realtor write up a purchase agreement?"

"I honestly thought about it, but I just didn't. And by the time I realized I'd been dragging out the process, it was too late. Two offers went out for it."

"Okay, so I have a question for you, and I want an honest answer. No matter what it is, I won't be upset. I won't blow you off, and I won't be a jerk."

She took a deep breath. "Okay."

There was fear in her eyes, so I attempted a smile to reassure her.

"My question is, did you not try for the house because you'd realized it wasn't right for you? Or do you not want to leave here?"

She started to look away again, so I caught her under the chin and forced her to look at me.

"Trust me," I whispered.

"I don't know," she said in a low voice.

I suspected she did, but she was scared. "What if I told you I don't want you to leave?"

Her jaw fell open.

"Man, those other guys did a number on you, didn't they?"

"The strong, independent woman in me says yes. But another part of me says I was the common denominator in all those relationships."

"I think you have bad taste in men, is all."

She lifted her brow.

I grinned. "Me excluded."

"But of course."

"Anyway, what if I told you that I like you being here? That I like you in my bed? And that I would like to see where this is going?"

"Aren't we doing it backward?"

"Fair point, but that doesn't answer my question."

She smiled shyly. "I would tell you that I like being here with you too."

"I thought so," I said with a little extra bravado.

She playfully shoved me. "Now, answer my question."

"Yes, it's a little backward, but speaking of backward, it seems silly for you to buy a house, only to fall in love with me and want to move back in two months later."

"You think very highly of yourself."

"I mean, the only reason you'd fall in love with me is because I fell in love with you first."

She blushed. I couldn't believe someone so open about herself and sex would blush at someone falling in love with her.

Paisley was going to need some extra care, but she was worth it.

"And if it doesn't work, I'm not going to treat you like those other men from your past. We'll replace your bed, and we can go back to being roommates until you find a new place to live," I offered.

"When you say it like that, it sounds so reasonable."

"I'm a reasonable guy. So, what do you say? Do you want to see where this goes between the two of us?"

"Yes."

"But that means no more rules."

She laughed. "Deal."

———

PAISLEY

As soon as Colin got in the shower, I pulled out my phone and texted my friends to tell them what had happened in bed that morning.

> Me: Am I crazy for saying yes? Am I going to ruin everything?

Elizabeth was the first to respond.

> Elizabeth: You weren't supposed to fall in love with your practice subject.

I couldn't tell if she was joking or not. She didn't often tease.

> Me: I didn't fall in love.

And I hadn't. When I thought back to my past relationships, I didn't feel for Colin what I had for them.

> Me: But I do like him. As more than a roommate and more than a friend.

> Alexis: I kind of agree with Elizabeth. You were supposed to work on not falling in love and then move on to someone else. HOWEVER, if you really like him, I think you should give you two a chance. And if it doesn't work out, consider it part of your experiment. Learn from it and move on.

I couldn't imagine losing Colin from my life and just moving on. That seemed kind of harsh. I knew that her ex-husband had done a real number on her, but I hadn't thought she was so cynical. She'd seemed to root for Bree's and Tessa's relationships, but thinking back, it was only after things had seemed to be good for them. Or maybe Alexis identified with me more. I really didn't know.

Tessa: Ouch. Colin's a person too.

Alexis: I'm not saying break his heart on purpose. I'm simply pointing out that Paisley needs to take care of herself first.

It was Saturday morning, Colin and I were heading into a real relationship, and his house was fixed. I didn't want my friends to fight over this.

Me: How about I worry about it if and when the situation arises?

Alexis: Just be careful.

Pru: We have your back, no matter what. Good luck to you both.

Me: Thanks, Pru. And thanks for worrying about me, Alexis. I love you too.

I shut off my screen and hoped that was the end of the conversation.

Chapter Thirty

COLIN

"HOW DO I LOOK?" I held out my arms, so Paisley could check out my suit.

She scanned me up and down, licked her lips, and whistled.

"So, you approve? I'm not too dressed up for the party?"

She shook her head. "You are just right. But you have to go back into the bedroom because you forgot something."

I looked down and felt my face. I'd already shaved, and I didn't see anything obvious in my clothes. "What did I forget?"

"I need you to fuck me first."

I grinned, stepped forward, and pulled her into my arms. "We don't need to go into the bedroom for that."

Slowly maneuvering her backward, I kissed her until we reached the wall. I drew one of her legs over my hip and brushed my fingers over the seam of her underwear. They were already damp, and she hissed. Pulling the material aside, I pushed two fingers inside her and rubbed them gently over her G-spot.

"More," Paisley commanded.

"Already soaked. Love that about you." I quickly unbuttoned my pants, lifted her, and drove inside her. I stopped for a second to appreciate no barrier between us and how incredibly good she felt, surrounding me.

But then she shuddered and opened her legs as wide as they could go in our current position, and I knew I couldn't hold off forever. She gripped the back of my neck, her fingertips digging in while I thrust into her over and over again.

By now, I knew the best angles and what made her come. Sometimes, it was just pushing inside her, but other times, I had to work for it. I might be an anomaly, but there were times that I liked having to earn it, like now.

Her legs began to shake, and her breathing grew shallow. I knew she was close. And if she went over the edge, I was going with her.

"Where do you want me to come?" I said into her ear.

That was the downside to no condoms, but if she wanted me to pull out, it would still be worth it.

"Inside me. Deep, deep inside me."

God. When she talked like that, I knew my time was almost up.

"If you want that, I'm going to need you to come first, baby." I kissed her neck. "Come on. Give it to me."

A sound that was somewhere between a moan and growl exploded out of Paisley's mouth as she came. Her already-wet pussy flooded with warmth and squeezed me tight.

I shoved inside, pinning her between the wall and my cock, and climaxed along with her.

We didn't get to enjoy much of an afterglow because I felt weak and my legs couldn't hold both of our weights much longer.

"I just left all my energy inside your pussy," I said as I set her down. "Mind if I stay home?" I joked.

Paisley smiled and reached under her dress to pull off her panties.

"What are you doing?" I had purposely only pulled them off to the side, so she wouldn't have to wrestle them back on.

She folded them into a neat little square and pushed them inside my pocket. "They're yours for the night."

I grinned. That was what I had told her the night we had dinner at my brother and sister-in-law's house.

I patted my side. "I guess I have to go now. Just in case you need them back."

She laughed. "Exactly."

If only I had been serious about staying home.

———

Paisley threw her arms around me. "Let's go dance."

I kissed her. "You're on your own this time."

Her bottom lip jutted out.

"Oh no, you already pulled that trick with me."

And it had worked. I'd already danced with her several times.

The engagement party was at a hotel. The couple had gotten a deal on one of the smaller rooms when they reserved one of the ballrooms for their wedding reception. And the location was giving me some inspiration.

"I have a better idea," I said. "How about we take a party break and sneak upstairs? It'll be like old times."

Paisley laughed. "That wasn't that long ago."

"It was in terms of our relationship."

"True. But I can't leave Bree's engagement party. She's my friend. Plus, we already had sex before we came."

"I get sex twice on the weekend, remember?"

Shaking a finger in front of me, she said, "No more rules, *remember?*"

"Dammit. What was I thinking?"

"I guess you weren't."

"What's going on here?" a feminine voice asked.

Paisley and I turned to see her friend Tessa and her husband, Seth, had approached us.

"Colin won't dance with me," Paisley said.

"Colin won't dance with her *again*," I corrected. "Colin has already danced with her."

Seth lifted his glass to his lips and chuckled behind it before taking a sip. Here was a man who understood where I was coming from.

"I'll dance with you," Tessa said.

Seth's smile fell, and he straightened his spine. "Are you sure you should be dancing?"

Tessa shot him a look. "Honey, I'm pregnant, not incapacitated. Dancing is fine." She turned back to Paisley and rolled her eyes.

Paisley laughed, took Tessa's hand, and took off for the dance floor. They made a beeline for the engaged couple, but as soon as Bree spun around and greeted her friends, her fiancé, Zack, snuck away.

When he saw Seth and me standing off to the side, he made his way over to us. "Hey, guys. Are you doing okay? Not bored or anything?"

I lifted my beer. "I'm doing good."

Seth raised his drink. "I'm good too."

Movement out of the corner of my eye caught my attention. The rest of Paisley's friends had joined her out on the dance floor. They were all laughing and looked like they were having a good time, but my eyes were for Paisley. She looked beautiful with the lights shining on her hair and the sheen on her skin. Even though she wasn't the best dancer, I was still mesmerized by her moves.

"So, it looks like another one bites the dust," Zack said.

"Huh?" It took me a second to realize he was speaking to me, but when I did, I had no clue what he was talking about.

Zack pointed to the ladies. "Paisley. And you. Another one bites the dust from their club. At this point, they're like dominoes."

Seth laughed, but I was still clueless.

"Club?" I asked.

"Yeah, their No Men, or I Hate Men, or whatever they call it club."

"United She-Woman Single Ladies with Our Vibrators So We Never Have Another Bad Date or Experience Romance Again Because Men Suck Club," Seth said.

"Damn, you know the whole title, huh?" Zack asked.

Seth shrugged and smirked. "I pay attention to detail."

"I get what you're saying, and I can appreciate that, man. But that's my little sister out there. I never kicked your ass for knocking her up, but one more sexual reference, and I just might," Zack warned, but he was half-smiling.

"Can we go back to the club thing?" I asked.

Zack frowned. "You don't know the ladies have a club where they all swore off dating men?" His eyes darted to Seth and back to me. "Paisley's never talked about it?"

"She mentioned that she wasn't dating and why, but she never said anything about her and her friends being in a club."

Seth cleared his throat. "It's not an official club. I think it kind of started as a joke."

"And obviously, they don't stick to it. Seth's already married to Tessa with a baby on the way, and Bree and I are engaged."

It was obvious that the guys were trying to make me feel better about not knowing.

"Yeah." It was weird that it had never come up between us though. "All her rules make sense now." She must have come up with them with her friends. I wondered what else they knew about our relationship.

"I heard about that," Zack said. He brightened. "And see, even though she didn't tell you flat out about the club, she basically told you aspects about it."

That did make me feel better.

For all of two seconds.

Zack looked out onto the dance floor again. "It was really nice of you to be Paisley's test subject to get her back into the dating game. Bree said she's come a long way at not falling in love at the drop of a hat."

My blood went cold, and Seth said, "Zack," in a stern tone.

Zack turned back to me, and my face must have given me away.

"You didn't know?" Seth asked, but it really came out more like a statement.

"No."

"*Fuck*," Zack said. "I thought with all the rules stuff, you knew the whole deal."

"Apparently not." I shoved my beer to Zack. "I think it's time for me to go."

I needed to think and go somewhere I didn't feel like an absolute fool.

Chapter Thirty-One

PAISLEY

AS MY FRIENDS and I danced, I noticed Bree's cousin Sebastian standing in the shadows, staring at Pru.

He looked like he wanted to eat her alive.

Pru didn't like Sebastian, so I didn't say anything to her, but I had to share what I was seeing with someone. I was getting hot, and he wasn't even staring at me, nor did I want him to.

I shook Bree's arm. When she looked at me, I pulled her close, so I could talk in her ear.

"Look at your cousin. I think he wants Pru."

"Yeah, to strangle her."

Sebastian didn't care for Pru either.

"No. Look." I gestured with my head to where her cousin was. Since he was facing us, I didn't want to point and have him notice.

Bree's eyes got huge. "Wow."

"Yeah. I guess he wants to strangle her while they have sex."

Bree laughed. "I guess so."

"Should we tell Pru?"

"Nah. I don't want a murder at my party."

It was my turn to laugh. "Good point." I sighed. "I wish someone would look at me like that."

"You're—"

"Bree."

It was Zack, and he looked like he had bad news. He whispered in his fiancée's ear.

"Zack needs to talk to us," Bree said.

I nodded, and we followed him off the floor. As soon as we were on the edge of the crowd, I scanned the room for Colin but didn't see him anywhere.

"Where's Colin?" I asked at the same time Bree said, "What's going on?"

"I fucked up," Zack said. "It seems, Colin didn't know about your little club. I think Seth and I convinced him it was nothing to worry about, but then I mentioned something about him being your test subject. Apparently, he didn't know that either. And he left."

"Shit." I took off for the table where my purse and phone were sitting. I quickly dialed Colin and stepped out of the room, so I could hear him better.

It rang several times.

"Pick-up-pick-up-pick-up-pick-up," I chanted.

Just when I thought he was going to ignore my call, he picked up.

"Yeah?"

"Please don't hang up," I begged.

He sighed. "What, Paisley?"

"Zack just told me what happened. Please come back, so we can talk about this." I could tell he was in his vehicle, so he could turn around and come back.

"I don't want to talk right now. And I think it's best you don't come to the house tonight."

Ouch. He said *the house* and not home.

Biting my lip, I wanted to plead with him to let me explain, but I also understood he needed time and space.

"Okay." I nodded. "I understand."

"Great."

"Maybe we can—"

The line went silent. I pulled my phone away to see the length of our call blinking at me. We'd talked for less than thirty seconds, and he'd hung up on me.

I had really fucked up.

———

COLIN

I was staring mindlessly into my fridge when there was a loud knock at my door. I sighed and closed the refrigerator. I'd been home for less than half an hour, and the woman couldn't even give me a few hours.

I marched over to the front door and swung it open. "Paisley, I said *not* tonigh—"

But it wasn't Paisley standing on my doorstep. It was Mateo with a case of beer in his arms and a bunch of other people behind him.

"What are you doing here?" I asked.

Mateo pushed past me. "The night is still young, you promised me a party, and since your date with Paisley fell through, I thought tonight was perfect."

I should have never called him, but I'd needed to talk to someone.

"Mateo."

He ignored me. "Come on in, everyone," he said.

Scotty and Leann were some of the first to enter.

"Sorry about your girl," Leann said.

"Mateo has a big mouth."

She smiled. "Yeah, he does. But we're still here for you."

"Thanks."

"You remember Clarice and Janie, right?"

Leann's friends stepped into the entryway.

"Hello, ladies."

They both smiled and said, "Hi, Colin."

"You remember my name, huh?"

Clarice put her hand on my shoulder. "We don't forget a pretty face."

I grinned. "Well, come on in."

Maybe a party wouldn't be so bad after all. It sure beat feeling sorry for myself.

Chapter Thirty-Two

PAISLEY

I FINISHED MAKING up Bree's couch as my bed and sat down, feeling the weight of the night on my shoulders.

"Sorry to ruin your party," I said to Bree. "But thanks for lending me some pajamas."

"You didn't ruin my party. It's not like you two had a fight and made a scene."

"Still, it ended on a bad note."

Bree sat down next to me. "You can blame my fiancé for that."

"No, you can blame me for that. I was the one who never told him about the club or...the other thing." I wasn't ashamed of keeping the club from him because it hadn't been done on purpose, but I felt incredibly guilty about him starting out as practice for me to not fall in love.

"Why didn't you ever tell him?"

"It wasn't like I was hiding it. It just never came up. I told him all about my situation with men and falling in love and not wanting to fall back into my old habits. I just never explained that the club was part of it. Especially since I still didn't know him that well at the beginning. It's one thing to tell him about myself, but I didn't need to tell him about all of us."

"Seems harmless enough. But..."

"But not telling him he was practice for me? Yeah, that was where I really messed up. I mean, he kind of knew since I gave him rules and explained why. Except..."

"Except he didn't know all your friends knew and that we actually had a secret plan for him?"

"Yeah. That." I groaned and covered my face. "What am I going to do?"

"I guess that depends on how you feel."

I dropped my hands. "What do you mean?"

"I mean, is this the end? Is this the point where your practice relationship has run its course? Obviously, I think you should talk to him, no matter what, because he deserves the respect, but is that where you end it?"

A cold chill went through me, and I shivered. I didn't like that at all.

"Or is this where you realize that you're in love with him and you can't live without him?"

"In love?"

"Yes. Like in all the romcom movies."

"Who are you, and what have you done with Bree?"

Just a few months ago, she had gagged at our monthly dinner because a guy proposed to his girlfriend in the restaurant.

"Ha-ha. I'm right here. And let's just say, I'm not so cynical anymore."

"I'm happy about that for you."

"Thanks. But you still haven't answered my question. Which is it?"

I shrugged. "Option C?"

"Explain."

"I don't want to end things with Colin. I know that for sure. He's a good guy, he's easy to live with, and he gets me. We've even been watching *Charmed* together." I smiled at the memory of him finding out that Leo was a White-lighter. He'd been shocked. "But I don't think I love him."

Bree tilted her head. "Why do you think that?"

I laughed. "Because this is me. I've been in love more than the rest of the club combined." It was a slight exaggeration, but I wasn't that far off. "I know what it's like to fall in love. And I just haven't felt that way about Colin."

"What if he called and said it was over right now?"

"Oh God." I put my hand on my chest. "I'd be very upset."

"And what if you saw him kissing another woman?"

I gritted my teeth. "I'd slap her so hard that she'd never even think about kissing another man again."

Bree nodded. "And what if I told you that I found the perfect house for you? Everything on your list is check-marked. And it's fifteen thousand less than what you want to spend?"

"I don't know." Her description should appeal to me, but it didn't. "It sounds great, but I like living with Colin."

"One last question."

"Shoot."

"Close your eyes and picture your wedding day. Who's standing at the altar with you?"

With my eyes shut, a grin spread across my face as I imagined Colin in a tuxedo. He would look so handsome.

"Yeah, you love him."

My eyes flew open. "You can't know that."

"Yes, I can."

"What about the other guys? This feels all kinds of different."

Bree grabbed my hand and squeezed it. "That wasn't love, honey. That was infatuation. Puppy love. Or maybe you just being in love with the idea of love. You never really loved any of them.

"By the way, at the party, when you said you wished someone looked at you the way Sebastian was looking at Pru? That's how Colin looks at you."

———

I blinked up at the ceiling and rolled over. I had fallen asleep after Bree went to bed but had woken up a half hour ago to use the bathroom, and I felt wide awake yet tired at the same time. I couldn't get comfortable, and at least part of what was keeping me awake was the guilt of hurting Colin.

Also, there was the fact that I missed him.

Maybe Bree was right, and I did love Colin. Maybe I

had never really experienced love before, and I'd just thought I had.

From another part of the house, a low moan traveled straight to my ears.

"Ugh."

I knew it was their engagement party night, but did Bree and Zack have to go at it all the time? To be fair, at least part of my frustration was jealousy.

I picked up my phone. It was inching closer to three in the morning with no messages or missed phone calls. Not that I had expected Colin to message me, but I still had been secretly hoping.

I knew that blue light and phones were a no-no before bed, but I had to do something to distract myself, so I didn't break down and call him in the middle of the night. And I was hoping it would make me sleepy again.

I scrolled through Instagram when I came across a familiar face. It was Colin's friend Mateo, and he looked like he was at a party or had been earlier. There were a set of ten pictures posted, so I scrolled through them, hoping he'd had a better night than I had.

But as I swiped left, a sinking feeling in my gut started and only got worse.

I recognized the house he was at. And picture nine was a selfie with him and Colin.

I gasped and sat up.

I quickly looked at the last picture. It was Colin again, this time with Leann. She was kissing his cheek while two other women were behind and above them, pushing their faces into the frame.

I checked the date, and they were posted with yesterday's date, and I knew it had to be correct. He hadn't hosted a party since he'd been home from England.

And then he'd had one last night.

I threw back the covers. There was no way I'd go back to sleep.

I needed to talk to Colin.

Chapter Thirty-Three

PAISLEY

I DIDN'T KNOW what I'd thought I would find when I got home, but it wasn't a quiet house. A part of me had still expected for there to be people drinking and partying, but all the main lights were off.

There was a light on over the stove when I got inside, and the streetlights were enough for me to see a figure on the couch. I had to unlock my phone to make out who it was though, and I hoped it was Colin.

It wasn't. It was Mateo, and as I headed to Colin's room, a pit began to form in my stomach.

When I had seen the Instagram post, I hadn't cared that Colin was taking a picture with Leann. I'd trusted him when he said that she was an old friend that he'd known for years. What had made me upset was that he'd had a party after what happened, and I was freaking out that I meant so little to him that he could have fun while I was miserable.

But for some reason, now that I was here, I had a voice in my head telling me not to open his bedroom door.

I put my hand on the knob but didn't turn it. I actually considered leaving, going back to Bree's, and pretending like I'd never come.

But I couldn't do that. I had to know.

I carefully turned the knob so as to make as little noise as possible and tapped the door open with my fingertips.

My breath caught.

The bathroom light was on with the door halfway open, giving me enough light to see Leann in Colin's bed with an arm slung over her waist. The sheet was covering from her breasts to her upper legs, but beyond that, I could tell she didn't have any clothes on. She was naked in Colin's bed. With Colin.

So much for just being friends.

Somehow, I managed to close the door as quietly as when I'd opened it and shuffled over to my room. It probably wasn't the best time to pack, but I didn't want to come back later.

I knew I had royally fucked up, but for him to turn around and sleep with someone else the same night broke my heart.

My own door was closed from what I assumed was for the party, and I scrambled to get it open before I started crying in the hall.

I made it just in time, my eyes filled with tears and my chest full with ache. I fell back against the wall and slid down it as the first sob escaped my body.

"Paisley?"

My head shot up, and I swiped my hands over my face to see better.

"Who's there?" I asked, my voice shaky.

I had gone from sad to scared. Being murdered would be the perfect ending to the last twelve hours.

"It's me."

I sucked in a breath at the voice.

"Colin?"

"Yes. What are you doing?"

I didn't answer. Instead, I burst into tears again and crawled in the direction of his voice.

I hit something that felt silky, like satin, and then his body underneath it.

"I'm in a sleeping bag," he explained. "I let Scotty and Leann have my bed."

I flung my body over his with relief that he hadn't moved on. "I'm so sorry."

"Shh, shh," he said and ran his hand over my head. "Why the tears?"

"You're too nice to me."

"You're crying because I'm too nice?"

I chuckled even though I was still crying. "No. I'm crying, *and* you're too nice. Not *because*."

"Why though?"

"I thought you were in bed with Leann."

"But I'm not."

"I know. I'm also crying because I want to be with you, and I ruined everything."

COLIN

"You didn't ruin everything."

She lifted her head and sniffled. "I didn't?"

"No."

"I'm so sorry about everything. I didn't tell you about the club because it's just this silly thing my friends and I came up with to make ourselves feel better. It's kind of embarrassing to tell people. But everything I told you about why I wasn't dating was true. I just failed to mention my friends were in on it too."

"I understand."

"And I'm sorry if I made you feel like I was using you. I'm so used to guys not caring about me and how I feel about them. When I first started things with you, I guess, subconsciously, I thought you'd feel the same."

"Yeah, after I calmed down and thought about it, I realized that I was maybe blowing things out of proportion."

That, and talking things over with Leann, Clarice, and Janie had helped me realize Paisley wasn't trying to hurt me.

"I'm still sorry."

"I know. And I accept your apology."

"Thank you," she said, laying her head on my chest.

"But you have to stop picking men who will reject you and pick guys like me. Guys who want to be in a relationship. Who want to be with you."

Paisley slid off me and onto the floor. She looked away. "That's what I've been trying to do."

"Yeah, I'm not sure about that. You got invested in a relationship with someone who wanted to stay friends. And you fell for someone who told you in his dating profile that he wanted to keep things casual."

"I told you way too much about my life."

I smiled. "Yet you forgot to tell me about two important things. Your club and that I was your test subject."

"Right." She sniffled. "I'm always messing up."

"Oh, Paise, you are not." I got up on my elbow and turned her face back to mine. "You just have a big heart, and the wrong people take advantage of that sometimes. I want you to be careful, is all."

"I understand." She put her hand over mine and shut her eyes for a second, as if she was savoring the moment. She nodded and sat up. "Thank you. And I hope you know that you deserve to be loved too. You deserve the wife and the family and the job that won't make you miserable."

"I know," I joked.

She chuckled, but it seemed forced.

"You okay?"

"Yes, but I'd better go. I was going to pack a few things, but I'll come back tomorrow when you're awake. And I'll find somewhere else to stay right away. Even though you said we're good, I think it would be awkward."

Suddenly, she burst out laughing. It had come out of nowhere, and it made me scared for her because I couldn't see anything funny with her talking about leaving.

I shoved the top of the sleeping bag off me and sat up. Grabbing her face, I leaned in close. "Paisley, what is wrong?"

"I'm such a screwup, Colin."

"No, you're not," I said sternly.

"Yes, I am. I know I'm supposed to take your advice, go out into the world, and tell myself I'm worth it. But everything—*everything*—I did to protect myself backfired. I ended up getting hurt again, and it's my own damn fault. The very thing I tried to prevent is the thing I made happen. I'm my own worst enemy. Don't you see how that's funny?"

"No, and I don't understand where this is coming from." I didn't understand what she was talking about. I'd already told her I forgave her.

She patted my cheek. "That's okay. It's my problem to deal with. But can you let me go? I don't want to start crying again."

I released her and sat back on my heels.

"And for the record, I'm not mad at you, but you did lie to me too."

"How's that?"

"You promised to help me not fall in love with you."

I tried to stop the grin from splitting my face in half, but I couldn't help it. "You love me?"

"Yes, but you don't have to be so happy about it."

I laughed. This woman always found a way to make me laugh. "I don't get it. I'm supposed to be sad? Disappointed? What?"

"I don't know." She got to her feet. "Anything but happy."

"I'm not supposed to be happy that the woman I love loves me too?"

"You love me?"

"Yes. I have since our first night together. Call me crazy, but I fell for you then, and if you hadn't been living in my house, I would have found a way to contact you to ask you out."

"Then"—her voice dropped to a whisper—"why don't you want to be with me?"

I threw my hands out. "When did I say I don't want to be with you?"

"You told me to stop picking men who will reject me. That felt like you telling me to do that in the future. As in we're no longer together."

"Woman." I scooped her up in my arms, laid her on the sleeping bag, and covered her with my body. "I meant, that is an important thing to keep in mind if something were to happen to us. But now that I know you love me, you're stuck with me forever."

"You need to be more specific. I'm emotionally fragile right now."

I kissed her. "My apologies. Will you ever forgive me?"

"Maybe."

"How about you crawl into my sleeping bag and let me make it up to you?"

"I'll think about it," she said, but the rubbing of her pelvis on mine told me she was already going to say yes.

"Just promise me one thing."

"What's that?"

"You'll still be here in the morning, and you won't leave me again."

"I promise."

Chapter Thirty-Four

COLIN

I TOOK a deep breath and knocked on my boss's door.

I'd only had two phone interviews so far, but I'd realized something this past weekend. If Paisley could face her fear of falling in love again, I could face telling my boss that I didn't want to do this job anymore.

"Come in."

Here goes nothing. I opened the door and stepped inside.

"Colin, what can I do for you?"

The bastard smiled as if he hadn't given me bad news the last time I was in there.

"I would like to put in my two weeks' notice. I can extend it to a month but only if you don't send me to St. Louis."

The look on Arnold's face was worth it. He went from shocked to pissed and back to shocked. "What the hell are you talking about?"

"I don't want to travel anymore. I have put in my time and have done it since I was hired. I've met someone, and I hope to someday start a family. I can't do that if I'm out of state more than I'm home. It wouldn't be fair to her or our future children."

"You've met someone?"

"Yes."

"But you're so young."

"I used to be but not anymore. And I'm tired of wasting my life on a job that doesn't care if I'm happy or not. So, it's time for me to go."

"What do you mean?"

"After going to a different country for a year, you were ready to send me off again for another long assignment without any consideration as to how it would affect me. So, I'm done."

Arnold stared at me.

"Anyway, let me know if you want two weeks or a month. I can do either. Or I can even go now if that's what you want." I grinned. *Thanks to my beautiful girlfriend.* She'd told me that if they let me go that day, she'd support us until I found another job.

I headed for the door.

"Five thousand more a year."

"I don't think you heard what I said about not traveling. No amount of money will get me to change my mind. I'm done."

I grabbed the door handle.

"Fine. Ten K more a year, and you can have Platt's job. He's retiring in two months."

I'd had no idea Roger Platt was retiring, or I would have asked for his job right away. And here I'd thought, I was going to have to quit to find a near-perfect job.

I schooled my face and slowly pivoted. "You have yourself a deal, but if you send me more than two hours away for extended periods, I'm done."

My boss curled his lip. "Fine."

"Nice doing business with you, sir."

I bolted from his office and to my own to call Paisley. I couldn't wait to tell her I wasn't going anywhere.

Epilogue

PAISLEY

"PAISLEY, I'm so happy for you," Alexis said. "I'm sorry I was so cynical about Colin."

"It's okay. I know your heart was in the right place." I picked up my menu. "So, what is everyone having?"

"Oh my God," Tessa said.

"Oh shit," Bree said.

I jerked my head up to see what my friends were looking at, and it wasn't good.

"Alexis," I warned, but she was already turning in her seat to see what Tessa and Bree were talking about.

I only had a profile view of her, but all the blood drained from her face as she saw her ex-husband with another woman. A very pregnant and young woman.

"That motherfucker," Pru hissed. "He won't give you the money for your half of the house, and now, we know why."

Alexis's ex-husband was supposed to sell their marriage home and give half of the proceeds to her. He'd been putting it off, knowing Alexis couldn't afford to take him to court again. Meanwhile, she'd been living in a small apartment, trying to save money for the bakery and café that she and Tessa had just opened.

The asshole had made her quit her job to stay home and had given her barely anything in the divorce.

Alexis spun back to us. "I think I'm going to be sick. That woman—" She covered her mouth.

"Honey, we saw," Bree said. "She's pregnant."

"And by the looks of that belly, she was pregnant before they were divorced," Pru said, crossing her arms and shaking her head. She looked like she was ready to kill the man.

"It's not that. I mean, it is, but..." Alexis said.

"What?" I asked gently.

"That's Candace."

I looked at my friends to see if they knew who Candace was, but they all shrugged.

"Who's Candace?" I asked.

But before Alexis could answer, Tessa gasped. "Oh my God, Candace was your exchange student."

Alexis and her ex had tried to get pregnant while married but had been unsuccessful. Now, it was a blessing she didn't have to share a child with the man, but at the time, it had been hard on Alexis. It was the reason she'd started baking.

The last year they had been married, to help ease the sting of not having a baby, they'd let a foreign exchange student live with them, and it looked like she had never left the US.

Alexis nodded, and someone gasped.

Pru slammed her fist against the table. "Let's turn him in."

"She was nineteen when she came to live with us. She's probably twenty now." Alexis shook her head.

"Dammit," Pru said.

"Are you going to be okay?" I asked.

She pushed her chair back and stood. "I need a minute."

"Do you want one of us to come with you?" Tessa asked.

She shook her head. "No. I'll be right back."

I stared after her. "Should we follow her even though she said not to?"

"No," Pru said. "Let's give her some space since that's what she asked for. But if she doesn't come back in five, one of us will go after her."

The six of us waited impatiently, but Alexis came back a few minutes later.

"Are you going to be all right?" Tessa asked as Alexis sat back down.

"As soon as I figure out how to get my money from him, I will be. I'm sick of that asshole jerking me around," she said, determination written on her face. "I know our little club is mostly a fun joke, but I'm so grateful for it and the six of you because I am *never* getting married again. That bastard has ruined me forever."

I knew that she was upset and was being very serious right now. But only one thought went through my head.

One shouldn't tempt fate.

Turn the page for a sample of
_____

NOT ANOTHER FAKE MARRIAGE

Not Another Fake Marriage

ALEXIS

The bell over the door to The Purrfect Café & Bakery rang, and I glanced that way for a second before returning to my task. I immediately looked back, but I must have imagined him.

"What's wrong?" Tessa asked as she continued to stock the display case with the pastries I'd just brought out to her.

"I thought I saw my ex-brother-in-law, but I think my eyes were playing tricks on me."

I didn't want to tell her, but ever since I had seen Kevin and Candace, I hadn't been able to stop thinking about him. Not because I wanted him back. That was never happening again.

No, it was because I was jealous. Not of Candace, but of my ex. I'd always imagined that I would have a beautiful family. With the man I loved and our one or two kids running around. But instead, I was alone and childless, and unless I decided to adopt, it looked like I was staying that way. It wasn't fair that my asshole of an ex-husband had gotten the house, the partner, and a kid.

Even though I'd said I was never getting married again, it still hurt.

I didn't even have a pet to call my own because my apartment was so small. I didn't think it was fair. I knew life wasn't fair, but in this instance, it should have been. The bad guy wasn't supposed to win at the end of the movie.

"Oh, Trevor? When's the last time you saw him?"

"Oh jeez. Probably a month or two before I left Kevin, so it's been a while."

"Maybe he heard about our place and came to check it out."

"Maybe." I doubted it though. Who would have told him? Kevin? I didn't think so.

What I did think was that I needed to stop dwelling on what my ex was doing and focus on what I had. A new business. And someday, I would no longer be living in a shoebox.

"The ladies and I have been talking," Tessa said.

"Oh? About what?"

"You."

"You've been talking behind my back?" I joked.

She grinned. "Is it behind your back if I tell you about it later?"

"Yes."

She laughed.

"What was the conversation about?"

Tessa's face got serious. "We think you should make a GoFundMe to get enough money to hire a lawyer and get the money Kevin owes you."

For a second, I let myself consider it, but I quickly shook it away. "I can't do that."

"Why? You said yourself you were going to do everything you could to get the money he owes you."

"That was when I was mad and full of fire. But it doesn't change my situation. By the time I got the money, it would probably all go to an attorney anyway."

"Which is why you start a GoFundMe."

"It's my mess, Tessa. I can't let others pay for it or take charity."

She looked at me skeptically. "Oh, really? But you could meet my husband behind my back and let him fund our café?"

I laughed. "He wasn't your husband yet. And he's a silent partner. Not the same thing."

"Then, let Seth be a silent partner in getting your money back from Kevin."

"Nice try."

Tessa's husband owned a very profitable advertising agency and could definitely afford to pay for my lawyer, but I wasn't going to ask him to do that.

"Okay, then let me."

"No."

"You have to do something," she said.

"I think I might be able to help with that," a deep voice said.

We both turned to see Trevor standing at our counter.

My mouth dropped open. He was really here, and he looked amazing.

He was two years younger than Kevin, but he looked at least five. Not that Trevor looked young. Kevin just looked old.

Trevor had thick, dark hair, a beard to match, and deep brown eyes. I'd forgotten how handsome he was.

Truth be told, it was Trevor I had liked first when I met the brothers. But it was Kevin who had made the first and only move, so he was the one I'd ended up dating. If only I could go back and say no.

"How can you help her?" Tessa asked, her voice full of suspicion.

"If you don't mind, I'd like to talk to Alexis about that. Alone."

"Um, sure. Why don't you come in the back with me? I need to check the timer on the oven anyway."

Trevor followed me back into the kitchen just as the timer beeped. I inspected the cupcakes and took them out of the oven.

"I have to admit, I'm pretty curious as to what you can do to help me." And why he was even in my café in the first place.

"Technically, I said I think I might be able to help with that."

I sighed. "You're as bad as your brother."

Trevor straightened. "I absolutely am not."

He was obviously offended, and I held up a hand.

"I apologize. I didn't really mean it. Kevin would often claim that he didn't say something. That I misunderstood or I got a few words wrong."

"So, he gaslit you?" Trevor shook his head. "What an asshole," he muttered.

"Yeah. That's the word for it." I faced the cupcakes and fiddled with them, so he couldn't see my cheeks turn red. I was both embarrassed that I had let someone treat me like that and validated that he had put into words what Kevin had done to me. When I could no longer stall, I turned back. "Anyway, how do you think you might be able to help?"

Trevor looked down. "My grandmother is dying."

I gasped. "Oh no." I had always liked Nana Nelson, even at the end, when she no longer came around. I was sure that Kevin had filled her head with stories about me, and I didn't blame her. Kevin was her grandson. "What's wrong?"

Trevor cleared his throat and lifted his eyes. "Cancer. Stage Four."

"I'm so sorry."

"Thanks."

"If there's anything I can do…"

"There is something."

This was a surprise. "Oh?"

"Did Kevin ever tell you about my grandfather's will

and how we needed to either be married or become a pharmacist to inherit the family business?"

"*That was true?*" I laughed at the ridiculousness of it. "I always thought he'd made it up."

"It seems like something he would do, but no, it's true. My grandfather was a spiteful bastard."

"I'll say. But what does this have to do with me?"

Trevor looked away. "I don't know how to tell you this, but Kevin is getting remarried to—"

"It's okay. I already saw them together."

The obvious relief on his face was almost comical.

"Then, you know, according to the will, Kevin will get everything. And he is planning to sell the pharmacy and let some developer bulldoze the place."

"Oh, Trevor. I'm so sorry."

"I'm glad you feel that way because I can't let my brother do that. And that's where you come in."

"Me?"

"Yes."

"What can I possibly do to help?"

"You can marry me."

About the Author

R.L. Kenderson is two best friends writing under one name.

Renae has always loved reading, and in third grade, she wrote her first poem where she learned she might have a knack for this writing thing. Lara remembers sneaking her grandmother's Harlequin novels when she was probably too young to be reading them, and since then, she knew she wanted to write her own.

When they met in college, they bonded over their love of reading and the TV show *Charmed*. What really spiced up their friendship was when Lara introduced Renae to romance novels. When they discovered their first vampire romance, they knew there would always be a special place in their hearts for paranormal romance. After being unable to find certain storylines and characteristics they wanted to read about in the hundreds of books they consumed, they decided to write their own.

One lives in the Minneapolis-St. Paul area and the other in the Kansas City area where they both work in the medical field during the day and a sexy author by night. They communicate through phone, email, and whole lot of messaging.

You can find them at http://www.rlkenderson.com, Facebook, Instagram, TikTok, and Goodreads. Join their reader group! Or you can email them at rlkenderson@ rlkenderson.com, or sign up for their newsletter. They always love hearing from their readers.